J
FIC
LAWREN– Lawrence, Caroline
CE
      The pirates of
      Pompeii

DUE DATE

THE PIRATES
OF POMPEII

Caroline Lawrence

The Roman Mysteries: Book III

THE PIRATES OF POMPEII

ROARING BROOK PRESS

Brookfield, Connecticut

Published by Roaring Brook Press
A Division of The Millbrook Press,
2 Old New Milford Road, Brookfield, Connecticut 06804
First published in 2002 in the United Kingdom by Orion Children's Books, London

Library of Congress Cataloging-in-Publication Data
Lawrence, Caroline.
The pirates of Pompeii / Caroline Lawrence. — 1st American ed.
p. cm. — (The Roman mysteries ; bk. 3)
Summary: At a refugee camp following the eruption of Mt. Vesuvius which buried
Pompeii, Flavia and her friends discover that children are disappearing and a very
powerful citizen might be involved.
[1. Kidnapping—Fiction. 2. Pirates—Fiction. 3. Slavery—Fiction.
4. Rome—History—Empire, 30 B.C.-476 A.D.—Fiction. 5. Vesuvius (Italy)—
Eruption, 79—Fiction. 6. Mystery and detective stories.] I. Title. II. Series.
PZ7.L425 Pi 2003
[Fic]—dc21   2002154482

ISBN 0-7613-1584-5 (trade edition)
2   4   6   8   10   9   7   5   3   1
0-7613-2604-9 (library binding)
2   4   6   8   10   9   7   5   3   1

Printed in the United States of America

First American edition 2003

To my husband Richard, who feeds me

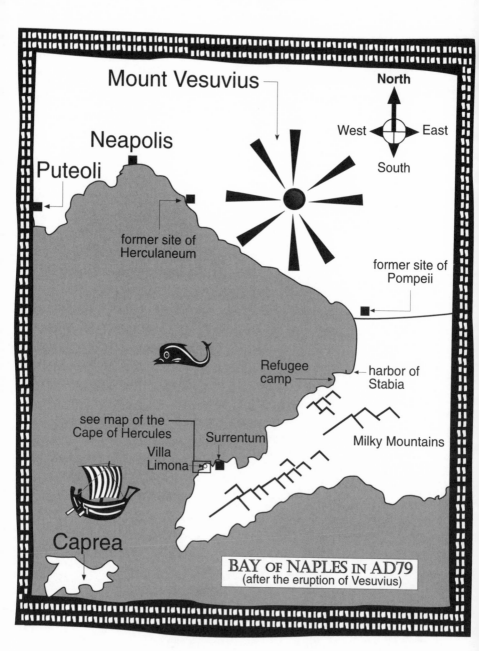

Mount Vesuvius

Neapolis

Puteoli

former site of Herculaneum

North

West — East

South

former site of Pompeii

Refugee camp

harbor of Stabia

see map of the Cape of Hercules

Surrentum

Villa Limona

Milky Mountains

Caprea

BAY OF NAPLES IN AD79
(after the eruption of Vesuvius)

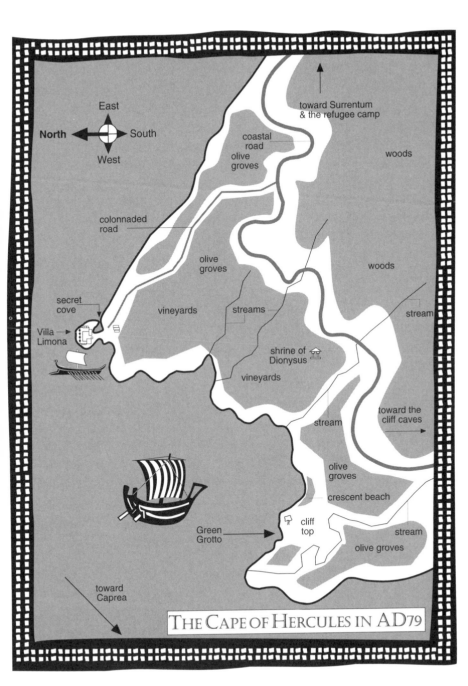

East
North ⊕ South
West

toward Surrentum
& the refugee camp

coastal
road
olive
groves

woods

colonnaded
road

olive
groves

woods

secret
cove

vineyards

streams

stream

Villa
Limona

shrine of
Dionysus

vineyards

stream

toward the
cliff caves

olive
groves

crescent beach

Green
Grotto

cliff
top

stream

olive groves

toward
Caprea

THE CAPE OF HERCULES IN AD79

This story takes place in ancient Roman times, so a few of the words may look strange. If you don't know them, "Aristo's Scroll" at the back of the book will tell you what they mean and how to pronounce them. It will also tell you a bit about patrons and clients in the Roman Empire.

THE PIRATES
OF POMPEII

SCROLL I

The mountain had exploded and for three days darkness covered the land. When the sun returned at last, it was not the same golden sun that had shone down on the Roman Empire a week before. It was a counterfeit, gleaming dully in a colorless sky above a blasted world.

On a gray hillside ten miles south of the volcano, a dark-skinned slave girl climbed a path in search of the flower that might save her dying friend.

Nubia turned her head left and right, scanning the ash-coated slope for a gleam of pink blossom. She did not know what Neapolitan cyclamen looked like, only that it was pink and had a remarkable ability to cure. The doctor had called it "amulet."

But there was no pink here. Only gray. Nubia climbed slowly past olive trees, figs, cherry, quince, and mulberry, all covered with the same soft crust of chalky ash. Here and there, black stumps showed where falling drops of fire had set an olive or palm tree alight. Some of the charred tree trunks were still smoking. It looked like the Land of the Dead, thought Nubia: the Land of Gray.

The blanket of ash muffled sound, but Nubia heard a cry drifting up from the beach below. She stopped, and looked back down. From this distance, the buildings around the cove seemed tiny.

Through the thin film of ash that still drizzled from the sky, she could make out the Inn of Pegasus on the right of the cove, by the headland. A few fishing boats—as tiny as toys—were drawn up on the beach near the boathouses where Nubia and the others had taken shelter from the eruption.

On the other side of the cove were the Baths of Minerva, the red roof tiles pale pink under a coating of ash. Between the baths and the boathouses were hundreds of tents and makeshift shelters. The refugee camp.

Another wail rose from the beach below and Nubia heard an anxious voice behind her.

"Who's dead? It's not him is it?"

Nubia turned to look at the girl with light brown hair who was hurrying back down the slope. Behind her, three dogs sent up clouds of ash as they pushed through the oleanders and myrtles on either side of the path.

"I don't think it is him," said Nubia, turning back to gaze down on the beach.

"Doctor Mordecai said he wouldn't live much longer . . ."

The girls watched a coil of black smoke rise from the funeral pyre on the shore. Around it, tiny figures lifted their hands to the hot white sky and cried out to the gods. Nubia shuddered and reached for her mistress's hand.

Flavia Gemina was more a friend than a mistress. A freeborn Roman girl, she had bought Nubia in the slave market of Ostia to save her from an unimaginable fate. Since then, Flavia's kindness had been like a drink of cool water in a desert of pain. Even now, Nubia took courage from Flavia's steady gaze and the reassuring squeeze of her hand.

After a moment they turned wordlessly and continued up the gray mountain, a dark-skinned girl and a fair-skinned one, wearing torn and dirty tunics, searching among the ashes for the plant that might save their dying friend Jonathan.

■ ■ ■

From the beach below, eight-year-old Lupus saw the girls start back up the path. They were easy to see: the only spots of color on the gray mountain. Flavia wore a blue tunic and Nubia a mustard-yellow one. The golden-brown dot pursued by two tiny black dots must be Scuto and the puppies.

Lupus was just turning back to the pyre to watch the body burn when he thought he saw something move much higher up the mountain. A person wearing brown. No. Two people.

Then a gust of wind blew acrid smoke from the funeral pyre into his face. His eyes watered and blurred. When he wiped then, he could still see the girls and their dogs, but the other figures had disappeared.

Lupus shrugged and turned back to the burning body.

The dead man's relatives were crying and moaning. Two professional mourners dressed in black helped the family express their grief with shrill wails. Lupus let their cries of pain wash over him. He didn't know who the dead man was. He didn't care. He only knew that the man's bloated corpse had washed up on the shore around noon. One of many in the past two days.

Lupus stood close enough for the heat of the flames to scorch him, and he kept his eyes open, though the smoke stung. When the professional mourners scratched their cheeks, he scratched his. It hurt, but it brought release. He needed to feel the pain.

The heat of the flames seemed to make the blackened corpse shiver, and for a moment, Lupus imagined it was the body of Pliny, the great admiral who had treated him with courtesy and respect, but who had died gasping like a fish.

Then the body became that of Clio, seven years old, bright, brave, and cheerful. Clio who he had tried twice to save. And failed.

Finally he saw the body of his own dead father. The father whose murder he had witnessed, powerless to stop. The father whom he had never properly mourned. Lupus tore at his cheeks again, and

3

let the pain rise up in him. Around him the mourners wailed. At last he, too, opened his tongueless mouth and howled with anger and grief and despair.

Flavia's keen gray eyes were usually excellent at spotting wild-flowers.

In Ostia, whenever Flavia went to visit her mother's grave out-side the city walls, she and her nurse, Alma, would gather herbs and wildflowers along the way. Flavia always left the prettiest ones at the tomb to comfort the spirits of her mother and baby brothers. Later, Alma would divide the remaining herbs into two groups. She used some for cooking and put the rest into her med-icine box.

When Doctor Mordecai had asked the girls to find amulet, Flavia had been confident of success. But now she found it hard to recognize the wildflowers beneath their covering of gray ash. By mid-afternoon, she and Nubia had found others that might be of use to the doctor: red valerian, doveweed and bloodblossom.

But no amulet.

So they continued up the mountain, climbing higher and higher. As they ascended, the olive trees gave way to chestnut, beech, and pine woods. The air grew cooler.

When they reached the summit, they stopped to catch their breath. Flavia uncorked her water gourd and took a long drink. Then she handed it to Nubia.

When Nubia had finished drinking, she wiped her mouth. It left a dark streak across her ash-powdered face.

"You look like a spirit of the dead," said Flavia.

"Don't say such a thing!" Nubia made the sign against evil. She poured some water into the palms of her hands and rubbed her face. "Better?" she asked.

Flavia nodded. Up here on the summit the ash was so thick that the puppies were up to their noses in it and had begun to sneeze.

Flavia lifted Jonathan's puppy, Tigris, and absently ruffled the top of his head as she looked around.

Ahead of them, across a level clearing among the pines, was a low wooden fence made of rough-hewn logs. Scuto bounded toward it sending up puffs of gray ash, mixed with pumice. Suddenly he stopped, looked back at Flavia, and whined.

The girls reached the rail at the same time. On the other side of it, the mountain fell away in a precipitous drop that made Flavia's stomach contract.

But it was the sight beyond that made her gasp.

From where they stood on the pine-covered ridge, Flavia and Nubia could see the great curving Bay of Neapolis on the left, the water scummy gray under an iron sky. Straight ahead, on the horizon, stood a terrible sight.

Vesuvius.

Its top half had been utterly blown away, leaving an ugly crater where the summit had once been. The edge of this crater glowed red, like a bloody, ragged wound. A plume of black smoke rose into the colorless sky and blurred away toward the southwest.

Below the smoldering volcano, a thousand fires burned across the chalky landscape, as if a vast besieging army were encamped at its foot. The smoke from the fires had created a dark transparent cloud that hung over the plain.

Flavia squinted and tried to find the landmarks she knew must be there: the port of Stabia, her uncle's farm, the town of Pompeii. Finally she found Stabia's harbor almost directly below them. She could make out the curved breakwater and straight piers and a few minuscule boats.

"Behold," said Nubia. "Villa of Clio."

"Where?" asked Flavia, putting down Tigris and shading her eyes. When the volcano had erupted, they had hurried to the Villa Pomponiana, the seaside house of their friend Clio. They had hoped to sail away, but had ended up escaping on foot.

"I don't see Clio's villa. Or Uncle Gaius's farm." Flavia frowned. "Where *is* the farm? It should be . . ."

"There," said Nubia, pointing. "Mound with smoke ascending heavenward."

Then Flavia saw it all.

Her knees went weak. She gripped the wooden rail at the cliff's edge and held on until her knuckles were white. For a horrible moment she thought she was going to be sick.

"It's gone," she whispered. "All of it. Clio's house, Uncle Gaius's farm and . . . the entire town of Pompeii. It's all been buried by the volcano!"

SCROLL II

The girls were halfway down the mountain when Scuto found something. The sun was sinking toward the sea and they needed to get back to the camp before it set, but his steady, urgent barking demanded their attention.

Presently the puppies joined in, echoing Scuto's deep bark with their high yaps. The girls left the path and wove between the gnarled and twisted trunks of ancient olives.

They found the dogs standing near a quince bush by the steep mountainside. Scuto stopped barking when they appeared and took a few steps toward them, tail wagging. Then he trotted back to the bush.

"Scuto! You found the amulet! Good boy!" Flavia knelt to hug Scuto around the neck while Nubia gently brushed ash from the tender blossom of a pink flower. Using a sharp stone, Flavia dug it out, careful not to damage the bulb.

"Behold!" cried Nubia, who had been searching for more amulet behind the quince bush.

The shrub hid the entrance to a cave.

"That's what they were barking at," said Flavia, putting the cyclamen in her shoulder bag and taking a step backward.

The cliffs and mountains of this region were honeycombed with caves. Flavia's uncle, Gaius, had warned them never to go in, reminding them that there were all kinds of wild animals in these mountains: foxes, wolves, wildcats, even bears.

Tail wagging, Tigris disappeared into the cave's dark mouth.

"Tigris," hissed Flavia. "Come back!"

From inside the cave came a piercing scream.

Flavia and Nubia exchanged horrified glances. Then, with a murmured prayer to her guardian gods, Castor and Pollux, Flavia ducked her head and plunged into the darkness.

The cave smelled of old smoke, musky animal, and urine. Before Flavia's eyes could adjust to the dim light, the high scream came again.

"No! Get the wolf away!"

Wolf! Flavia's instinct was to turn and run, but Nubia was close behind her. Then Tigris's bark rang out, unnaturally loud in the confined space.

Now Flavia could see a small figure huddling at the far end of the cave about five feet away, and near it, the shape of a small black wolf.

Flavia laughed. "It's just Tigris. He's a puppy. He won't hurt you."

She took another step into the cave, crouching because of the low roof. Nubia followed, and as she moved away from the entrance, the orange light of the setting sun poured in, illuminating a little girl who wore a torn tunic and one sandal.

Shivering in terror, the child pressed herself against the back wall of the cave as the dogs snuffled around her toes.

"Scuto. Tigris. Come here at once!" said Flavia sternly. "You, too, Nipur." The cave was low at the back, and Flavia had to approach the girl on hands and knees.

"Don't be afraid. We won't hurt you. What's your name?"

The little girl gazed up at Flavia with large tear-filled eyes. Her nose was running and she stank. Flavia guessed she had wet herself with fear.

Flavia pulled her handkerchief out of her pouch and put it under the girl's nose.

"Once for Castor," said Flavia brightly.

The little girl blew obediently.

"And once for Pollux."

The girl blew again.

"That's better, said Flavia. She tucked the handkerchief back into her belt and sat cross-legged on the dirt floor of the cave.

"My name's Flavia Gemina. This is Nubia, and these are our dogs. Scuto's the big one. The puppies are Tigris, the brave one, and Nipur, the sensible one. What's your name?"

The little girl sniffed. "Julia."

"How old are you, Julia?'

"Five."

"Where are your mommy and daddy?" Flavia asked.

Julia's chin began to quiver and her eyes welled up with tears again.

"Don't worry," said Flavia hastily. "It doesn't matter. Whey don't you come outside with us now? We'll try to find them."

Julia put her thumb in her mouth and shook her head vigorously.

"Come on! It will be dark soon."

Julia shook her head again and said in a tiny voice: "Rufus said for me to wait here."

"Who's Rufus?"

"My big brother. He told me to wait here when the men were chasing us. He told me not to go away. He promised he would come back."

"What men?" asked Nubia softly. She had been crouching by the door. Now she moved forward and squatted beside Flavia.

Julia looked at Nubia and her eyes widened.

"You have black skin!" she whispered.

"Nubia's from Africa," explained Flavia. "Haven't you ever seen an African before?"

The little girl shook her head again, still staring at Nubia.

"Who were the men chasing you?" asked Flavia patiently.

"The scary men," whispered Julia, and her lower lip began to quiver again. "Rufus told me to hide here and wait for him. He told me he would come back soon. And then he didn't come and it's been a long time."

"Did you spend the night here?" asked Flavia.

Julia shook her head and tentatively reached out to stroke Tigris, who was sniffing her big toe.

"Are you thirsty?" asked Flavia, holding out the water gourd.

Julia nodded and took the gourd. She drank in long gulps and then handed it back, gasping.

"Come on," said Flavia brightly. "It's nearly time for dinner. I'll bet you're getting hungry. We'll leave Rufus a message telling him where you've gone. OK?"

Julia nodded absently. She was busy petting Tigris, who sat beside her with his eyes half closed.

On the way down the mountain, Julia became quite chatty.

She told Flavia that she and her brother, Rufus, were staying in the refugee camp with their grandparents. They had gone to search for early apples or figs. Then the scary men had come out of the bushes. Two of them. One had grabbed her and one had grabbed Rufus. But Rufus was brave and had kicked one so hard that he had fallen to the ground.

Julia took a breath and continued.

"Then I screamed my loudest scream and bit the other one on the arm and Rufus kicked him between the legs and then we ran and ran up the mountain and I couldn't run anymore and then we could hear the men behind us and Rufus saw the cave and said, 'Wait here. Don't move. I'll be back.' But he never came back."

"Well," said Flavia, "if he does come back he'll find the message I wrote in the ash outside the cave. You're sure he can read?"

Julia nodded. "He goes to school," she said in a small voice, and then stopped on the path. "What if the scary men caught him and he never comes back?" Her brown eyes started to fill with tears again.

Flavia knelt in front of the little girl. "We'll find him, Julia," she said. "Nubia and I are very good at solving mysteries. I promise you we will find your brother and bring him back to you!"

SCROLL III

The sun, enormous and bloodred, began to sink into the sea. Its dying rays lit the ash-covered mountains and cove, so that the whole landscape seemed to be bathed in blood. The sky above it was livid purple, the color of an angry bruise. There would be no stars that night.

In the camp, people moaned and wailed at the evil omen of a bloodred world. Some believed that Apollo, the sun god, was dying and that he would never rise again. Others were convinced that the end of the world was days away, or maybe only hours. They called out to their gods, they tore their clothes, and they sprinkled ash on their heads.

But among the wails of despair were shouts of joy. An old man and woman were hurrying toward Flavia and Nubia as they came down from the mountain.

"Julia!" cried the woman. "My baby!" Her hair was streaked with gray, but she lifted her skirts like a girl and ran across the beach.

"Grandma!" Julia threw herself into the woman's arms. Scuto barked and jumped up and down and the puppies raced after him.

The old man ran straight past Julia and her grandmother. He was tall, with a lined, leathery face and thinning gray hair. He looked around wildly, glancing only briefly at the girls and then beyond them.

"Rufus?" he cried. "Rufus?"

Now Julia's grandmother was on her knees hugging Julia and kissing the girl's hands in tearful gratitude.

The old man looked at Flavia. "Where's Rufus?" he cried. "Where's my grandson?"

He must have seen the answer on her face. Before Flavia could explain, he ran up to the road and cried out in a hoarse voice, "Rufus! Rufus! RUFUS!"

Nubia's family had always lived in tents, so she had been able to help her friends put up one of the best in the camp. It was made of an old ship's sail, several cloaks, and a large blanket, purchased from the owner of the baths, a chinless Etruscan named Scraius.

Scraius had consented for Doctor Mordecai to convert the palaestra into a hospital and the solarium into a surgery. He also let the refugees use the toilets and fill their water gourds and jars at the seven pipes that brought mineral water down from the mountains. He could afford to be generous: A steady stream of people passed through the baths from dawn till dusk, bringing more business than he'd ever had before. The steam room was being repaired, but the hot room and cold plunge were still in use, as were the three mineral pools.

Scraius had also allowed the doctor to pitch his tent against the outer colonnade of the baths, so he could be near his patients. Just inside the entrance of their tent, by one of the columns, Mordecai's daughter Miriam had scraped a depression in the sandy ground. Then she had surrounded this hearth with flat stones and filled it with coals. Now she knelt over it, stirring a delicious-smelling stew in an earthenware pot. Nubia recognized the pungent aroma at once: goat.

In the dim interior of the tent, Flavia's tutor, Aristo, was lighting candles. With his curly golden-brown hair and smooth tanned skin, he always reminded Nubia of a bronze statue of the messen-

13

ger god Mercury that she had once seen in the market of Ostia. Aristo looked up at the girls and smiled.

The girls smiled back but went straight to Jonathan, who lay on a low couch, the only one in the tent. The girls stood looking down at him and Flavia asked, "How is he?"

"No better, I'm afraid." Mordecai sat cross-legged on a rush mat beside his son. "Did you find the amulet?"

Flavia nodded. "Only one. Scuto found it. I hope it's enough. And there are some other herbs you might be able to use . . ."

"Thank you, Flavia and Nubia. And Scuto." Mordecai accepted the cloth shoulder bag with a little bow of his head.

"Would you girls like some stew?" asked Miriam.

"Yes, please," said Flavia. "We're famished."

"It is goat?" asked Nubia.

Miriam nodded. "Goat and chickpea."

Rush mats and cloaks had been spread over most of the sandy ground to make the floor of the tent. Flavia sat on one of the cloaks beside a man with hair the same color as hers.

"How are you, Uncle Gaius?" she asked.

"My ribs hurt like Hades, but Doctor Mordecai says that means they're healing." He smiled ruefully, and then winced. The robbers who had cracked his ribs had also bruised his jaw and broken his nose. Beside him an enormous black wolflike creature gnawed a bone.

"How is the Ferox?" asked Nubia, kneeling to stroke the big dog. Once Ferox had been the terror of Stabia. But he had almost died trying to protect his master, Gaius, from horse thieves, and a knife wound in the chest had rendered him harmless as a lamb.

Ferox wheezed at Nubia, rolling his eye and thumping his big tail twice on the blanket. Then he returned to his bone.

"He had goat for dinner, too," observed Nubia.

"Where did you get it?" asked Flavia.

"I bought it with the last of my gold," sighed Mordecai. "The vendor was asking a fortune."

"Father gave half the goat meat to that poor family in the tent next to us," said Miriam proudly, ladling a spoonful into one of their two bowls.

"Miriam," chided her father gently, "we are told not to boast about our giving, or we lose the blessing."

"Sorry, Father."

Flavia frowned. "How will we buy food now?" she asked.

"God will provide," said Mordecai quietly.

There were only two wooden bowls and no spoons, so the girls used pieces of soft flat bread to spoon the hot stew into their mouths. When the bread grew too soggy, they ate the gravy-soaked morsels.

"Goat was delicious, Miriam," said Nubia, using a last piece of bread to wipe the bowl clean. She reached for the water gourd and took a long drink. The water was cold and fizzy and smelled of egg. It was so full of iron that it turned their tongues rust-red. When Nubia had finished, Flavia took the gourd.

"Mmm," said Flavia. "I'm getting used to the taste of this water."

"It's very good for you," said Mordecai. "People come from all over Italia to take the waters here." He looked down sadly at Jonathan. "If only you would drink some, my son . . ."

"Behold!" said Nubia suddenly. "His eyelids butterfly."

"Yes," whispered Mordecai. "I believe there are moments when he is closer to waking than sleeping. Flavia, pass me the water gourd, please."

Mordecai took the gourd and dribbled a few drops onto Jonathan's cracked and swollen lips.

"Drink, my son," he said. "Drink and live."

But the water merely dribbled down the side of Jonathan's pale cheek and he did not wake.

SCROLL IV

"Lupus!" cried Nubia as the boy came into the tent. "What is happened to you?" There were red scratch marks on his cheeks.

Lupus shrugged. His eyes were red-rimmed and his face smudged with soot, but Nubia thought his green eyes look calmer. He went straight to his friend Jonathan, lying as still and pale as a corpse, and looked down at him. After a moment Lupus turned away in silence and sat heavily beside the girls.

Miriam filled a bowl with stew and placed it on the rush mat in front of Lupus.

"We've all eaten," she said. "This is yours." She handed him a piece of bread and a water gourd.

From the corner of her eye, Nubia watched Lupus eat. He had no tongue and they all knew a careless bite could be his last. He chomped with his molars and threw his head back to swallow. If he wanted to chew on the other side of his mouth, he had to tip his whole head to one side. When he drank, he held the gourd at a distance and expertly directed a stream of water to the back of his throat.

Nubia saw the others staring at him openly. Sometimes they forgot that he hated to be watched.

"What is news?" she asked Mordecai, hoping to distract them.

"Two more deaths." Mordecai was grinding the amulet to a paste using a long smooth stone and the second wooden bowl. "When people have no reason to live, they choose to die. One man was not very ill at all."

"And a boy is missing," said Miriam. "A boy named Apollo. His mother was looking everywhere for him."

Nubia gasped and looked at Flavia.

"That's strange," said Flavia. "Nubia and I found a little girl named Julia hiding in a cave in the mountains. She said some scary men chased her and her brother. And now *her* brother is missing, too."

"Is the little girl all right?" asked Miriam.

Flavia nodded and Nubia explained. "We take her to grandma and grandpa's tent nearby."

"Maybe her brother was the same boy. The boy named Apollo." said Gaius.

"No," said Flavia. "Julia's brother is called Rufus."

"There is no end of men's wickedness." Mordecai shook his head. "A terrible disaster befalls us and immediately man's evil nature reveals itself. The villagers here have been asking huge prices for old blankets and food and cups and bowls. People strip the bodies that wash up on the shore of rings and jewelry before they can even be identified. It was only a matter of time before some wicked person thought to take advantage of the confusion by kidnapping children, no doubt to sell them into slavery."

"We're going to find out what's happened to the children," said Flavia. "I promised Julia. I just need to think how to go about it. . . ."

Nubia wondered if Mordecai would object, but he was busy smearing the amulet paste onto Jonathan's dry lips.

There was a pause, broken only by Lupus's chomps and smacks. Then a note, the sound of a string being plucked.

Aristo held a tortoiseshell lyre on his lap. He was tuning it by tightening the ivory pegs that held the strings.

"A lyre!" cried Nubia. "Aristo, where are you finding it?"

"Scraius, the owner of the baths, loaned it to me. He says he rarely plays it. It only needed a little tuning." Aristo strummed the strings. A chord swelled and then died.

"Will you pluck song for us?" asked Nubia.

"I will play if you will play."

"I will play." Nubia pulled the lotus-wood flute out from beneath her mustard-yellow tunic. It hung on a silken cord around her neck, always close to her heart, for it was her most treasured possession.

"Good," smiled Aristo. "You begin, and I will follow."

Jonathan was hunting in a green walled garden that stretched as far as the eye could see. He grasped his bow in his right hand and heard the reassuring rattle of arrows in the quiver slung over his shoulder. In his belt was his sling, and there were seven smooth stones in his pouch. The cicadas in the olive grove zithered a song and the sky above was as blue as turquoise. There was a scent of wild honey in the air.

His puppy, Tigris, ran ahead, sniffing the sun-dappled trail and looking back every so often to make sure his master was following. Jonathan could not remember what they were hunting, but he trusted Tigris. Presently his puppy left the olive grove and raced down a grassy hill. Now Jonathan could really run, and he almost flew. Something was different, and suddenly he realized what it was. Usually when he ran he had to fight for air. But now it felt as if his sandals were winged, like those of the messenger god Mercury.

There was no tightness in his chest, and he ran as he had never run before.

Tigris led him to a broad river, clear as crystal, with trees on either side. Jonathan stopped and stared. The fruit of the trees glowed with colors he had never seen before. And on the other side of the river was a city made of jewels, too vast and complicated for his mind to comprehend.

"Jonathan," said a voice. "Go back. The children need you."

The bloodred sun had been extinguished by the sea, and black night fell upon the camp. The swelling moon and stars were hidden by ash and cloud, but on the beach yellow fires burned and hearths glowed red.

The camp was full of restless noise. People still wailed and moaned, only a little less now that their bellies were full. Couples argued, children cried, and babies whimpered. But as Nubia began to play her flute all these sounds faded.

She played the "Song of the Lost Kid." And as she played, she touched those she loved.

Nubia had named each of the eight polished holes under her fingertips after a member of her family. The deepest note was father-note. Then came mother-note. Her mother's voice had been low and rich, full of warmth and laughter. Then came the Taharqo-note, named after her eldest brother, who, at sixteen, was the best musician in the clan. It was he who had taught her the "Song of the Maiden" and the "Song of the Lost Kid." Then came Kashta-note. Kashta was her cousin. Although he was only thirteen and had not yet undergone the coming-of-age ceremony, he already seemed to Nubia to be a man. If she still lived in the desert she knew she would soon be betrothed to him.

Then came the higher notes. The Shabaqo- and Shebitqo-notes. They should have been the same, for Shabaqo and Shebitqo were twins, but Shebitqo had been born second and was a little smaller, so he was the higher of the two notes. Then she fingered the Nipur-note, named after her dog, and finally, the Seyala-note. Seyala had been Nubia's little baby sister, so young she was not out of the sling.

As Nubia played the flute, it was as if her fingertips caressed each one of those she loved, those whom she would never see again. Each note was a voice calling to her from the past begging her not to forget. Tears wet her cheeks, but when she played, she touched her family, so she didn't mind.

As Nubia played, she heard Aristo first strum, then pluck the translucent strings of the lyre. Her music was sad, but his was full of hope. It filled her with hope, too, and her sad song became sweeter. Then Lupus found a beat somewhere and pattered it softly on his upturned wooden bowl.

SCROLL V

As the music took wings and began to soar, a movement caught Flavia's eye. The red cloak, which served as their tent door, had been pulled aside and a small girl stood in its opening.

In the instant before Julia let the flap swing closed, Flavia saw dozens of people standing in the darkness outside the tent, as still as statues.

Julia ran across the tent floor and sat heavily in Flavia's lap. She leaned back against Flavia's chest, put her thumb in her mouth, and watched Nubia play her lotus-wood flute.

Flavia saw Mordecai give Miriam the merest nod. Jonathan's sister stood and unpinned the red cloak. It slipped to the ground, opening their tent to the west.

A great crowd of refugees stood gazing in at the musicians. They were utterly silent. In the darkness of the night, with the thin ash swirling around them, they looked like ghosts from the underworld.

As Nubia, Aristo, and Lupus played on, Flavia saw glints of light and heard tiny thumps. Some of the refugees were tossing coins into the entrance of the tent.

"Remarkable," Flavia heard Mordecai murmur. "These people barely have enough money for bread, yet they're willing to spend their precious coins on music."

■■■

The music guided Jonathan back. The notes of the flute were cool and clear: silver, green, and blue. The lyre was sweet and warm: honey, damson, and cherry. The drum wove the sounds of the two instruments together into a carpet of many colors. This musical carpet slipped under him and supported him and lifted him with joy.

Suddenly Jonathan was flying. Flying on the music.

He was flying over silk. Wrinkled indigo-blue silk. There were tiny dots on the blue fabric. He flew lower and saw that the dots were tiny boats and that the wrinkles on the silk were slowly moving.

He was not flying over cloth.

He was flying over water.

The music helped him stay aloft. It supported and it guided him.

Now he was flying over a ship with a red-striped sail. On its deck he could see children running back and forth. He flew over a gold and green island with two peaks, then over the deep blue water again and along a rugged coast.

As he rode upon the musical carpet, the coastline became grayer. Presently he slowed. Below him was a blue cove, a crescent beach, olive trees dusted with what seemed to be dirty snow, a few boats, tents, people, lots of people. People fishing, washing, cooking, talking. And among them . . . among them a thin bearded man walking through the crowds and pushing aside the flap of a tent. His father.

Inside the tent it was dark, starred with candle flames and the red glow of a coal fire. There were people here, some playing music, and his father sat beside a dark-haired boy on a low couch. The boy looked thin and pale.

His father's head was bent, the long gray hair pulled back at the neck. His father looked strange and vulnerable without his turban.

Floating above this scene, Jonathan suddenly felt a clutch of horror. The boy he was looking down on was himself!

He must go back into that thin, weak body.

He didn't want to.

He loved flying over the sea and over the islands. He loved the strength and joy he had felt hunting in the garden. His father and others would be with him soon. Then they would understand. They would not want to leave paradise either.

The music stopped as the musicians put down their instruments for a moment.

His sister's voice in the dim tent: "Don't stop playing the music. I think I saw him move! I think the music is bringing him back."

Then Flavia's voice. "Don't die, Jonathan. We miss you. Tigris misses you. Come back to us. . . ."

"Please, Lord, bring him back," prayed Jonathan's father, and then: "Play a little more, please, Nubia."

Nubia raised the flute to her lips.

But already, in his heart, Jonathan had whispered: "Yes."

Suddenly he was engulfed in dry pain. He felt unbearably hot, and his head throbbed. There was a strange taste in his mouth. They were all standing over him and around him. Too close. No space. Tigris's wet tongue was cool on his hot cheek. He could smell doggy breath and he could feel someone's hand gripping his so hard it hurt.

Now the memory of flying and of paradise began to slip away, like water from a cracked cup. No, he cried out silently in his mind, don't let me forget.

Then he shuddered and gasped, and there was only a terrible all-consuming thirst.

"He's awake!" squealed Flavia. "Jonathan's awake!"

Lupus uttered a whoop. Nubia dropped her flute and clapped her hands. Miriam burst into tears.

"Praise God!" whispered Mordecai, bending close. "How do you feel, my son?"

Jonathan blinked, as if even the dim candlelight hurt his eyes. He tried to speak but his lips were cracked and swollen.

"Water. He needs some water," said Mordecai. But Miriam was already at her brother's side with a water gourd.

Miriam wiped the tears from her cheeks and gently held her brother's head. Then she put the gourd to his lips.

Jonathan drank only a little water, then he laid his head back on a scorched silk pillow. He murmured something.

"What?" said Mordecai. "What did you say?"

"Water. Tastes funny," croaked Jonathan weakly. "Like fizzy eggs."

"Yes," smiled Mordecai. "This is an Etruscan spa town. Famous for its mineral waters. Miriam gave you the sulphur water. It's good for you."

"Sulphur bad," whispered Jonathan. "Killed Pliny."

"Yes," said Mordecai. "This region has many underground caves full of sulphur gas. Too much of it is deadly, but a little bit is good for you."

"You should try the iron water," said Flavia. "Its turns your tongue red."

"And magnesium-num," attempted Nubia. "Tastes like dung of camel."

Jonathan frowned blearily at the African girl. "How do you know what—? No, don't answer that. . . ."

They all laughed and Flavia said softly, "Welcome back, Jonathan."

Nubia went to sleep happy that night. Somehow Jonathan had woken from his deathlike sleep. The night was hot, but she was used to heat. And there was something comforting about sleeping in a tent on soft sand. It reminded her of home. Nevertheless, or perhaps because of this, she had terrible nightmares.

She dreamed the slave traders came again, wearing turbans that covered not just their heads but their faces, too, so that only their eyes were visible. In her dream they all had one evil dark eye and one white blind eye, like Venalicius the slave dealer. The one-eyed men slashed at her tent with sharp, dripping swords and then set it on fire.

Nubia woke herself trying to scream.

Stars. She must find the stars.

Hugging her woolen cloak about her, Nubia rose, slipped out of the tent, and lifted her eyes to the sky.

When Venalicius had carried her far across the Land of Blue to the Land of Red, the only familiar thing had been the stars in the sky. At Flavia's house she had slept in the inner garden with Scuto, comforted by his furry warmth and by the familiar constellations overhead. But tonight she could see no stars. Tonight there was nothing to remind her of home and who she had been.

"You play very well." A low voice in the darkness made her start. "What clan are you from?"

At first Nubia thought she was still dreaming; the voice was speaking her native language!

Then she saw the white gleam of his eyes and teeth.

"I was listening in the shadows," he whispered. "Your music brought me down from the cave."

"Who are you?" whispered Nubia.

"My name is Kuanto of the Jackal Clan, but here they call me Fuscus."

"I haven't seen you in the camp."

"Nor will you." His voice sounded just like her eldest brother's. "I am the leader of a band of runaway slaves."

"A slave! But if they find you . . ." She gave an involuntary shudder. Nubia knew that the Romans crucified runaway slaves. She was not sure what "crucified" meant, only that it was something terrible.

"But they will not find us," said Fuscus quietly. "Our masters are dead. Buried under the ash of the volcano, along with our past. This disaster has given us the perfect opportunity to start a new life."

Then he moved a little closer, so close that the warm breath from his mouth touched her ear and sent a shiver down the side of her neck.

"I have come to ask you to join us," he whispered. "Run away with us, and be free again."

Years of sleeping in graveyards had taught Lupus to be a light sleeper. His ears were keen as a rabbit's and his vision sharp as an owl's, as if the gods had compensated him for the loss of his tongue.

He crouched at the entrance of the tent and watched as the man gave Nubia something. Then he saw her remove one of her tiger's-eye earrings and give it to him in return. Lupus could hear almost everything they said to one another. Unfortunately, he did not understand one word of the language they were speaking.

When Nubia slipped back into the tent and lay down again beside Flavia, he was already back in his own sleeping place, pretending to be asleep.

But long after Nubia's breathing became low and steady, Lupus remained awake, staring into the darkness with open eyes, and thinking.

SCROLL VI

Flavia was determined to solve the mystery of the missing children, but she and her friends were so relieved to have Jonathan back that for the whole morning they barely moved from the tent. They took turns giving Jonathan sips of water and chicken soup and telling him what had happened while he had been in the deep sleep that Mordecai called a coma.

The last thing Jonathan remembered was the death of Pliny.

"Well," said Flavia, "we left him there on the beach and went up to the road and walked and walked. We made it round the promontory and took shelter in the boathouses with lots of other people. The night seemed to last forever and we thought it was the end of the world."

"Then sun appears," said Nubia.

Flavia nodded. "The next day Pliny's sailors and slave went back to get his body. Tascius and Vulcan went with them. They wanted to go back to Herculaneum to try to find Clio and her sisters and her mother."

Lupus hung his head. He and Clio had become very close and Flavia knew he feared she was dead, so she hurried on.

"The old cook Frustilla died of breathing sulphur—"

"—like the Pliny," interrupted Nubia, and added, "and almost you."

"The funeral pyre on the beach has been lit every day." Flavia shuddered.

"Many bodies wash up onto the naked shore," said Nubia quietly.

Lupus held up both hands, fingers spread.

"And your father?" Jonathan croaked. Flavia's father was a sea captain who had set sail from Pompeii two weeks earlier.

"He should be safe in Alexandria," she said with forced brightness. "He wasn't planning to get back until the Ides of September."

Flavia took a deep breath.

"Jonathan," she said. "You must get better quickly, because we have a new mystery to solve. Two boys are missing from the camp: one named Apollo and another named Rufus. Your father thinks someone may be kidnapping them to sell them as slaves. We've got to find out who's doing it and rescue them before it's too late."

Jonathan frowned.

"Yes," he whispered. "While I was asleep I think I dreamed. Something about saving children. I can't remember exactly. But I know it was important."

Lupus slipped from tent to tent, listening hard. Jonathan was sleeping and Flavia had asked him to start collecting information while she and Nubia finished their chores. He knew how to make himself look extremely ordinary so that most people hardly noticed him. To them he was just an eight-year-old boy in a grubby tunic, playing in the sand.

At first there had been over two thousand people in the refugee camp. Most thought they were going to die and spent their days praying to the gods to spare them or take them quickly. But gradually as the falling ash began to thin, they realized it might not be the end of the world. Some families set off north to see if they could rebuild their lives. Others headed south to stay with relatives and friends.

In the past two days almost three hundred people had packed up and left.

Lupus sat on the shore near a fishing boat. He pretended to be engaged in a private game of knucklebones. On the other side of the boat two fishermen were mending their nets and chatting quietly. He couldn't see them but he could hear them perfectly. And he could see most of the camp. He was watching one family in particular. They had dismantled their makeshift tent of blankets and were preparing to leave.

The father was a stocky dark-haired man. He carried most of their belongings on his back. The mother was short, with frizzy hair. She was wearing black, as if she'd been in mourning even before the eruption. There were three girls, the youngest of whom was about Lupus's age.

"Melissa!" the father was shouting. "Melissa!" The girls were calling out, too: "Melissa, we're going!" They had been calling for some time now, their voices growing louder and more urgent.

"By Jupiter!" scowled the father, "Where is that girl? I told her not to go far!" He angrily shrugged his bulky pack of blankets to the sand and stalked off toward the water. The mother wrung her black shawl distractedly and the girls looked miserable.

Then Lupus heard something that puzzled him. One of the fishermen on the other side of the boat said under his breath, "Looks like Felix just got luckier."

"Poor little minnow," replied his friend.

"Best to forget you even heard it," said the first, and they continued mending their nets.

It was just past noon when Miriam pulled aside the cloak doorway and the dim light in the tent brightened. Nubia put her finger to her lips and Flavia whispered a greeting. Jonathan was still asleep. The girls had been filling water jars and gourds from the water spouts outside the baths. They had just brought the last one in.

Nubia could see that Miriam was exhausted from helping her father in the hospital all morning. But she still looked radiant.

"We just delivered a baby," whispered Miriam, her violet eyes shining. "It's so wonderful to see new life after all the death around us."

She sat on some of the scorched cushions they had taken from Tascius's villa and carefully untied the blue scarf around her head.

On the night of the eruption, a fragment of burning pumice had set Miriam's dark curls on fire. Some of her hair had gone up in flames and part of her scalp had been burned. As she gingerly uncovered it, Nubia could see that the burn was still ugly and red. The hair over her right ear would probably never grow back.

Miriam reached wearily for a small clay jar of balm and removed the cork with her elegant fingers. Everything about Miriam had seemed perfect to Nubia, especially her beauty. But now that perfect beauty was marred.

Nubia rose from Jonathan's side and went to Miriam.

"Here, let me," she said, and took the ceramic jar. She dipped her finger in the balm and stroked it very gently onto the ugly red burn.

"Oh, that feels wonderful," sighed Miriam, and closed her eyes. "Thank you, Nubia." After a moment she said, eyes still closed, "Are you going to try to find the missing children?"

"Yes," whispered Flavia. "Lupus was just here. He wrote us a message: A girl named Melissa has disappeared."

Miriam opened her eyes and frowned.

"Lupus managed to get a piece of her clothing," continued Flavia. "He's gone back out with Scuto and the puppies to see if they can track the scent. We're just about to go, too."

"Poor little creature!" sighed Miriam, and closed her eyes again. She looked as if she were in pain. When Nubia had finished smoothing the ointment onto her burn, Miriam lay back against the cushions. Almost immediately her breathing became slow and steady and the frown on her smooth forehead relaxed.

The girls glanced at each other, then back at the red burn on the side of her head.

"Will her hair ever be growing back?" whispered Nubia.

"I don't think so," said Flavia. "I think she'll always have a scar."

"So sad," said Nubia. "The perfect beauty gone."

The subdued light around them grew brighter again as Flavia's uncle Gaius stepped into the tent, then it dimmed again as he let the cloak fall back.

Both girls put their fingers to their lips and pointed at Miriam.

He nodded, smiling. He'd obviously been to the baths because his light brown hair was damp and he smelled pleasantly of scented oil: balsam and laurel.

Ferox opened both eyes and thumped his tail again. Gaius limped over to his dog and lowered himself carefully onto the soft floor of the tent. He ruffled Ferox's head and scratched behind his ear, but he was gazing at Miriam, asleep on her cushions.

The swelling on Gaius's face was going down, but his nose would be permanently crooked and he still had one black eye. Yet there was such a look of compassion on his battered face that it brought a lump to Nubia's throat. She glanced at Flavia and Flavia smiled back.

Nubia knew they were both thinking the same thing: Miriam's beauty might be marred for others, but for Gaius it would always be perfect.

"Come on, Nubia," whispered Flavia, "let's go and see how Lupus is doing."

"Yes," said Nubia. "Let's see how Lupus does."

Flavia spotted Lupus leaning against a palmetto tree in front of the Inn of Pegasus. The innkeeper must have brought a bowl of water for the dogs because they were lapping thirstily. Lupus saw the girls coming and shook his head to say the dogs hadn't been able to find a scent. He was chomping something and guiltily tried to hide it behind his back as they came up.

"Hey, Lupus! Where'd you get the sausage?" Flavia could smell it.

He looked embarrassed.

"From me," said a voice from the shadowy doorway. The innkeeper stepped out. He was tall and thin with bony elbows and knees, and moist brown eyes.

"I read your young friend's message," he said.

Lupus flipped open his wax tablet and showed it to the girls. On it he had written neat letters:

DO YOU KNOW ABOUT MISSING CHILDREN?

"We're looking, too," said Flavia.

"You're doing a good thing, trying to find the missing children," said the innkeeper, who smelled faintly of vinegar. "But you'd better be careful. You don't want to get captured yourselves." He reached into a jar on the counter just inside the doorway and brought out two more sausages.

"Thank you," said Flavia taking them. She handed one to Nubia and took a bite of the other. It was deliciously spicy. "How do you know about the missing children?" she asked with her mouth full.

The innkeeper shrugged. "Everyone knows about them." Then he lowered his voice. "And some people suspect who is behind it."

"Who?" said Flavia eagerly.

The innkeeper glanced around. "I know who you are," he said. "Your uncle has paid for three poor widows and their children to lodge here, and the doctor is treating the people of this camp *gratis*. So let me give you some advice. This part of Italia is far from Rome. Things are done differently here. There are some people with great power," he lowered his voice, "power almost as great as the emperor's."

"Who?" asked Flavia again.

"These men of power are like spiders," said the innkeeper. "Their webs are almost invisible and they're everywhere. And like spiders, they are not afraid to bite."

"But who?" said Flavia for the third time.

"Let's just say there is one particular man and he is . . . fortunate. Very fortunate. Most of the crime in this whole area, from Neapolis to Paestum, can somehow or other be linked back to him. They call him the Patron." The innkeeper licked his lips nervously and looked over Flavia's shoulder. She glanced back. Some fishermen were making their way up to the inn from the beach.

"Be careful of the spider and his web," whispered the innkeeper and gripped Flavia's wrist with his bony hand. "One other thing," he said. "There is a rumor that a gang of runaway slaves is on the loose in the area. You know what happens to runaway slaves. If they are recaptured, their lives are not worth living. They will do anything to keep from being caught again. Anything. Do you understand?"

Flavia nodded.

"I must be careful, too." The innkeeper backed into the shadowy interior of the tavern. "But I will help you if I can. My name is Petrus."

SCROLL VII

That evening Nubia noticed the crowds gathering outside their tent even before sunset. As well as coins, some people shyly left gifts at the entrance: loaves of bread, an embroidered belt pouch, a carved wooden beaker, some dried figs wrapped in laurel leaves, a handful of olives.

"What's happening?" said Jonathan, as Flavia came in from the baths. He was propped up against all the cushions. "Why are all those people outside our tent?"

"Nubia, Aristo, and Lupus played music last night," said Flavia, "while you were still in a coma."

"The people are hungry for more than bread and olives," said Mordecai. "They long to feed their souls with music."

He turned to Nubia and Aristo. "Your music is as important as my medicine. Will you play again tonight?"

"Of course," said Aristo. He began to unwrap the lyre from its protective piece of linen.

Nubia nodded and pulled the flute from beneath her tunic.

"Hey!" cried Flavia., "That red cord on your flute is new, isn't it? Where did you get it?"

Nubia's heart skipped a beat. Before she could think of an answer Flavia said: "Oh, I know! Someone left it as a gift. Don't look so worried! Keep it; you deserve it."

34

Miriam rose gracefully to her feet and unpinned not only the red cloak doorway but the dark goat's hair blanket that formed one side of their tent. The interior of the tent was now completely open to the west. A few yards from the new tent opening stood many children and adults. Their backs were turned on the blood-red sun that had terrified them the night before.

As Aristo began to tune his lyre, a hush fell over the crowd.

Nubia noticed Lupus lying on his stomach in the darkest corner of the tent.

"Lupus," she said, "will you drum us?"

Lupus tried not to smile, but Nubia could tell he was pleased. Carrying his wooden soup bowl, he sauntered over and sat between them.

Aristo finished tuning his lyre and Lupus turned his bowl upside down. They both looked at Nubia. She closed her eyes for a moment and then lifted the lotus-wood flute to her lips.

As the sun sank into the sea, she began to play.

Flavia loved the music her friends were making. It made her think of sunnier, happier, greener days. She closed her eyes and let the music guide her to those times.

She didn't know how long she had been listening when a small hot body landed in her lap.

"Oof!" gasped Flavia, jolted from her reverie. Then she smiled. It was Julia, damp and clean and with her thumb in her mouth. Flavia put her arms around Julia and the girl snuggled tighter, her back against Flavia's front and her hard head under Flavia's chin. Flavia kissed the top of the little girl's head and smelled the sweet warm fragrance of her silky hair.

Julia was quiet after that and Flavia closed her eyes again and let the silent tears come.

When at last the music died away, it was very dark.

There was a long pause.

"No, don't stop!" someone cried out of the silence.

"One more song," called out a man.

"Aristo, we love you," came a girl's voice.

Flavia and Jonathan exchanged surprised looks.

"Wait!" A man in a brown tunic stepped into the dim firelight. "You've cried with the music, now laugh with our comedy!" he proclaimed dramatically.

Two torchbearers—one short and one tall—appeared on either side of him and the sandy ground was flooded with light. Flavia couldn't see the announcer properly because he had his back to them.

"I am Lucrio," cried the man in a well-trained voice, "and I would like to present Actius and Sorex, famous actors of repute and renown. They will present for your enjoyment a short comedy of their own composition: *The Pirates of Pompeii*. . . ." Here the announcer stepped aside and made a theatrical gesture.

The torchbearers fixed their torches in the sand and stepped into the torchlight. They bowed toward the audience. Then they turned to bow to the musicians: Nubia, Aristo, and Lupus.

As they lifted their heads, Flavia saw that they wore brightly painted comic masks with huge leering grins.

In her lap, Julia stiffened. Abruptly the little girl let out a scream so shrill it brought all four dogs to their feet. Everyone in the tent turned toward Flavia and she saw their faces in the torchlight staring at her wide-eyed. Julia was still screaming but now she had twisted around and buried her face in Flavia's shoulder. As she began to cry, Flavia heard the little girl sob over and over, "The scary men! The scary men!"

"How was *The Pirates of Pompeii*?" Flavia asked Jonathan the next morning as they ate breakfast on the beach. She had spent most of the evening helping Julia's grandparents calm the hysterical little girl back at their tent.

Lupus mimed applause.

"It wasn't bad," Jonathan said. "It was the usual story of clever slaves, rich but stupid young men, and children captured by pirates. Those two actors played all the parts."

"Oh," said Flavia, disappointed. "Sounds good."

It was Jonathan's first time out of bed since he had woken. The four friends sat by the water's edge, watching the little waves deposit more ash on the sand. They were eating their breakfast: tangy goat's cheese and flat bread. The three dogs sat attentively nearby.

"It was hard to tell because of their masks, but I think the actors were angry that they didn't make as much money as Nubia, Aristo, and Lupus," said Jonathan, gesturing with a piece of bread.

"Probably because it wasn't the best choice for a comedy," said Flavia. "Pompeii has been buried and children are missing."

Lupus nodded and Flavia tossed a morsel of cheesy bread to Scuto, who caught it in midair with a snap of his jaws.

"Jonathan!" she cried.

"What?"

"Do you think they were trying to tell us something, like the innkeeper was? Only they . . ." she tried to think of the word, ". . . they *disguised* it, so that it wouldn't be obvious?"

"Yes," he said slowly. "We never thought of *pirates* taking the children, but that would explain why they completely disappear!"

"And look!" said Flavia, indicating two strong fishermen pulling their boat up onto the beach. "These boats come and go all the time, but we never take any notice of them. . . ."

"What do you think, Lupus?" asked Jonathan. "Could it be pirates who are taking the children?"

Lupus pursed his lips and nodded thoughtfully, as if to say he thought it was very possible.

"Nubia?" said Flavia, and glanced at the slave girl.

But Nubia's amber eyes were directed upward. For the first time in days the chalky white sky had a tint of blue to it.

"She's miles away," said Jonathan, feeding his last scrap of bread to Nipur. "Miles away."

"OK," said Flavia, as they strolled back to the tent. "Here's the plan for today. Lupus, you patrol the beach. Watch all the boats that come and go. Keep an eye out for any unusual behavior. Jonathan, you go to the baths and see if you can overhear anything."

"Good idea," said Jonathan. "I haven't had a bath in over a week."

"I know. That's what gave me the idea." Flavia grinned at him. "Nubia and I will find those actors from last night and . . . Great Neptune's beard!"

They all stopped a few yards from the red flap of their tent. Two Roman soldiers in dazzling armor stood on either side of the entrance. They both held spears and they both stared straight ahead.

Flavia glanced at her friends. Then she set her jaw and took a step forward.

In perfect synchronization the two spears crossed, blocking the entrance.

"Hey!" cried Flavia. "That's our tent!"

Keeping his gaze on the horizon, one of the soldiers growled: "And you would be?"

"Flavia Gemina, daughter of Marcus Flavius Geminus, sea captain!"

"Well, Flavia-Gemina-daughter-of-Marcus-Flavius-Geminus-sea-captain," said the soldier with the hint of a twinkle in his eye. "There's a very important person in there at the moment and you'll just have to wait until he comes out."

A clink of armor sounded from the other side of the tent flap and the two spears pointed up again. Flavia and her friends jumped back as two more soldiers emerged from the tent and stood at attention. Then a bull-necked man with receding sandy hair ducked out through the tent's opening.

He blinked in the light and looked down at Flavia and her friends. Short and stocky, with a pleasant face, he looked strangely familiar to Flavia. He reminded her of Brutus, Ostia's pork butcher. However, the richly embroidered purple toga draped around his shoulders showed he was no butcher.

Flavia's jaw dropped as she looked from the gold laurel wreath on his head to the heavy gold wrist guards on his arms and down to his gold-tooled leather sandals. She knew why his face seemed so familiar: There was a marble bust of him in her father's study.

"You must be Flavia Gemina," he said mildly. "I heard you introducing yourself to my guard. I believe we are distantly related. I am a Flavian, too."

He extended his ringed hand for her to kiss.

Flavia nearly fainted.

She was standing two feet away from Emperor Titus!

SCROLL VIII

Scuto wagged his tail as Flavia dutifully pressed her lips to the hand of the most powerful man in the world. The emperor's thick fingers were laden with gold rings and the back of his hand was soft and freckled.

"Flavia," said her uncle Gaius, coming out of the tent with a tall gray-haired man, "the emperor has come to our rescue. He has brought food and wine and blankets and medicine. And he wants to see Doctor Mordecai."

"Um . . . he should be in the infirmary," Flavia stuttered and the others nodded, wide-eyed.

"Lead on," said the emperor, throwing out one arm in a sweep of purple.

Flavia, Jonathan, Nubia, and Lupus led the most powerful man in the Roman Empire across the sandy ground, through two columns, and into the solarium. The dogs knew from experience that they were not allowed in the baths; they flopped down panting near the entrance.

The solarium was bright and cool. Its outstanding feature was a picture window of tinted green glass facing north toward the bay.

Miriam, her dark curls bound up in a blue scarf, was talking and laughing with a woman on a massage couch. She looked up as they entered and when she saw the soldiers and emperor, her face went pale and she quickly handed the baby back to his mother.

Someone must have told her the emperor was in the camp, for she immediately went to him, knelt, and kissed his hand.

"Beautiful," breathed the emperor as he helped her to her feet. And then frowned. "Have we met before? You look very familiar. . . ."

Miriam lowered her eyes and gave her head a slight shake.

"Miriam," said Gaius, "the emperor is looking for your father. He's not in the tent. Is he here?"

"He was here a moment ago," stammered Miriam. "I'm not sure where he's gone. . . ."

"Shame," said the emperor, swiveling majestically on one foot and looking around at the airy room with its frescoed walls and high blue ceiling. "Reports of his good deeds reached me in Rome even before I set out for the region. I wanted to personally encourage him in his work."

"I'm sorry," said Miriam again, and Flavia thought she looked unusually flustered.

"Don't be, my dear." The emperor smiled, revealing a row of small white teeth. "Why don't you take me around the patients? I should like to speak to them."

"Of course," said Miriam, and led him toward the new mother, who clutched her baby tightly in a mixture of terror and delight.

"Oh, Flavia," said Gaius, "I've haven't introduced you to Pollius. He's one of my patrons. He buys more of my wine than anyone else in the region. He lives a few miles south of here, in Surrentum."

Flavia turned from the emperor to the man standing beside her uncle. At first she thought he was old, because his hair was mostly gray. Then she noticed his tanned face was as smooth and unlined as Aristo's. He couldn't be much older than her father. But the most striking thing about him was not the contrast of his smooth tanned face and graying hair.

It was his eyes.

Although they were unremarkable—dark and slightly too close together—when he turned them on Flavia she felt a strange thrill.

Her uncle was gesturing for Miriam to come over. With a nervous glance at the emperor, who was speaking to the young mother, Miriam slipped away to join them.

"And this is my betrothed." Gaius took Miriam's hand and for a moment they gazed into each other's eyes as if no one else existed. Then Gaius remembered himself.

"Miriam, this is one of my patrons, Publius Pollius Felix. He's a close friend of the emperor. He's been taking him on a tour of the devastated area."

"Hello." Gaius's patron gave Miriam the same direct look he'd given Flavia. He had a light cultured voice.

Flavia studied the gray-haired man. He was tall and clean-shaven, like her uncle, and very handsome. But there was something else about him. Something she couldn't describe. The thought suddenly occurred to her that he was really the emperor, and the bull-necked man in the purple robe was an impostor.

She felt a tug on her tunic and turned, irritated. It was Lupus. He was making bug-eyes at her, as he did whenever he wanted to communicate something important. He tipped his head toward the door.

Jonathan and Nubia were staring at her, too.

"Um, Uncle Gaius," said Flavia. "We'll go and find Doctor Mordecai."

"Good idea," said her uncle with a smile turning back to his patron.

"What is it?" hissed Flavia when they were outside again. They moved along the portico, beyond earshot of the emperor's guards.

Lupus took out the wax tablet he carried everywhere and opened it with a flick of his wrist.

His notes from the previous days were still etched into the yellow wax on the left-hand leaf.

Flavia took it and frowned as she read it out loud.

GIRL MISSING. MELISSA.
"FELIX JUST GOT LUCKIER."

"You told us this yesterday. That's what the fishermen said."

Lupus nodded urgently.

Jonathan cleared his throat. "I think what Lupus is trying to tell us is that a man named Felix might be involved in the kidnappings."

Lupus nodded.

"And?"

"Didn't you hear your uncle?" said Jonathan. "His patron's name is Felix."

"Great Neptune's . . ." gasped Flavia. "And *felix* means 'lucky' or . . . fortunate!"

"The innkeeper!" shouted Jonathan, and then clapped his hand over his mouth. Lupus was nodding vigorously.

Jonathan continued in a whisper: "You told me the innkeeper said most of the crime in the area can be linked back to a very fortunate man!"

"Wait!" said Flavia, holding up her hands. "Wait, wait, wait. Before we get too excited . . . Felix is quite a common name, isn't it?"

"I suppose so . . ." said Jonathan.

"Felix slave name," offered Nubia.

"She's right," said Flavia. "Lots of slaves are called Felix."

"But that man is no slave," said Jonathan. "He has three names. And I don't think he can be a freedman. Did you notice the gold ring on his finger?"

"No. But he must be rich if he can afford to buy lots of my uncle's wine."

"And he's a close friend of the emperor," said Jonathan. "You can't get much more powerful than that. Do you think he's the man they call the Patron?"

43

Flavia nodded slowly. "I'll bet he is. The innkeeper said the fortunate man had power almost as great as the emperor's. And he is my uncle's patron."

The four of them looked at each other.

"I have a plan," said Flavia. "It probably won't work, but if it does it will be very dangerous. Are you willing to try it?"

Without hesitation, the other three nodded.

"Good. But first, we have to be sure that man is the one the innkeeper thinks is behind the kidnappings. Wait here and make sure he doesn't go anywhere. I'll be right back!"

Flavia ran as fast as she could across the ashy beach, dodging children, skirting tents, leaping over smoldering campfires.

The Inn of Pegasus was closed because it was only mid-morning, but the door was not locked. A serving girl directed Flavia to a cool musty storeroom built into the cliff itself. The innkeeper was decanting wine from a large amphora into smaller jugs.

It was dim in the storeroom, but light enough for Flavia to see the innkeeper's expression when she told him breathlessly that the emperor was in the camp.

Petrus looked surprised and pleased.

"And he's here with my uncle's patron, a man called Felix," she added.

"Publius Pollius Felix?" said Petrus.

Flavia nodded.

The look on his face told her all she needed to know.

SCROLL IX

Publius Pollius Felix was still in the solarium with her uncle Gaius, watching as Titus made his circuit of the sick and injured. The emperor had just found a veteran soldier who had served with him in Judaea and the two of them were deep in conversation.

Aristo and Miriam were changing the bandage on a burn victim in a far corner of the room.

And Mordecai was nowhere to be seen.

"He's not back yet?" said Flavia breathlessly to her uncle. "We couldn't find him anywhere. He must have gone to someone's tent."

"That's a pity," said Felix, "because the emperor has to leave soon. I'm accompanying him to Stabia, where a warship is ready to take him back to Rome." He turned to Gaius, "I'll return this afternoon to help distribute the blankets and food. It would be useful if you could tell me which of the refugees are in greatest need."

"Of course," said Gaius. "I'll make up a list. Jonathan, are you all right?"

Jonathan had put his hand to his forehead and was staggering a little.

"Yes," he said weakly, "just hard to breathe . . ."

Suddenly he fell back, unconscious.

Flavia and Nubia were standing right behind him. They caught him neatly and lowered him to the floor.

"Is he ill?" said Felix, taking a step forward and looking down at Jonathan with concern.

"He's very asthmatic and the ash in the air is bad for him," said Flavia. "He almost died of it. He only came out of his coma yesterday."

Felix looked sympathetic.

Flavia coughed. "It's hard for Lupus, too," she said, "because when he was younger someone cut out his tongue and all the ash gets down his throat. And Nubia's throat is still sore from the iron collar she had to wear when she was enslaved." Flavia coughed again and glanced pointedly at Lupus and Nubia, who coughed, too.

"By Jupiter!" exclaimed Felix. "You children have had a bad time of it."

Jonathan stirred and groaned. His eyelids fluttered convincingly.

"I told Jonathan he should go where the air is fresher," said Flavia solemnly, "but he said he didn't want to take his father away from the important work he is doing here."

"This boy is the doctor's son?" said Felix.

Flavia looked up at him and nodded. She tried to make her eyes look big and innocent. For a long moment Felix's dark eyes held her gaze and she wondered if he had seen through their ruse.

Then Felix turned to Gaius.

"Flavius Geminus, old friend," he said. "Why didn't you say something sooner? I have a huge villa in Surrentum with plenty of spare rooms. Send your niece and her friends to stay with me for a few days while we sort out the refugees."

"Well," stammered Gaius. "It never even occurred to me. Wouldn't it be a terrible imposition? Four children? Not to mention their dogs . . ."

"Not at all," said Felix with a faint smile. "I have three daughters, the eldest about the same age as your niece . . . I insist that they come to stay with me at the Villa Limona."

"I'll have to ask Jonathan's father," said Gaius, "but I'm sure he'd be delighted. Thank you, Pollius Felix, thank you very much. I don't know how I shall ever repay you. . . ."

"Don't think of it." Felix placed his aristocratic hand on Gaius's shoulder. "That's what patrons are for. Perhaps someday I will call upon you to do me a small service in return."

Before the emperor departed, he climbed up onto his imperial carriage and gave a short speech to all those in the camp. He had been an army commander and Jonathan could hear every word perfectly.

Nearly two thousand refugees listened in silence as the emperor promised to compensate those who had lost property or possessions, to find and return lost children and runaway slaves, to help them rebuild their lives.

"Many of you will be worried about friends and relatives buried in the ash or trapped in buildings that have collapsed," said the emperor. "It may ease your minds to know that even as we speak, an entire legion is combing the affected area, searching for survivors."

There was a huge cheer, but as it died down Jonathan overheard a man tell his wife that so far they'd found no one alive.

The emperor continued: "Those of you who have documents to prove you own property buried by the eruption—be it land, slaves, or animals—should present them to the official scribes tomorrow. If you do not have documentation, two or three witnesses will do. I promise that I will do everything in my power to compensate you. Even if I have to reach into my own purse to do it!"

This statement received the biggest cheer of all. There were shouts of "Hail Caesar!" and "May the gods reward you!" Many of the refugees were in tears, but Jonathan noticed a few exchanging skeptical glances.

47

"My agent for this area," the emperor continued, "is Pollius Felix." He gestured toward the gray-haired man, who stood nearby. "He lives a few miles south of here and has assured me that he will visit the camp regularly. If you have any special problems or disputes, take them to Pollius Felix."

Shortly afterward, the imperial carriage drove north up the coastal road. The Praetorian Guard followed on horseback.

The plume of gray ash had barely settled when Mordecai appeared at Miriam's side.

"Father!" cried Jonathan. "Where have you been? They've been looking everywhere for you! The emperor was here. He wanted to thank you!"

"God forgive me, I could not face the man," said Mordecai. "I cannot forget what he did.

"But Doctor Mordecai," protested Flavia. "He promised to help everyone who's been hurt by the volcano."

"He brought many food and blankets," said Nubia.

"And he told us," added Jonathan, "that you had done the empire a great service. He wants to reward you."

Mordecai looked at his son from his heavy-lidded eyes. "That man has the blood of ten thousand Jews on his hand," he said, "including that of your mother."

"How?" said Jonathan. "How is the emperor connected with Mother's death?" It was noon, and for the first time since the eruption the sun had broken through the ashy cloud cover. They had moved to stand in the thin shade of the colonnade.

"Nine years ago," said Mordecai heavily, "he was the commander of the legions that destroyed Jerusalem. It was Titus who gave the command to burn the temple. Thousands of our people died in the siege of Jerusalem. Among them your mother."

They all looked at each other in dismay.

"There are even those," continued Mordecai, "who say that he is the reason Vesuvius erupted. The rabbis always said God's curse would come upon this land if ever Titus rose to power."

"And I kissed his hand," whispered Flavia with a shudder.

"No," said Mordecai, patting Flavia's shoulder. "I'm not asking you to hate him. I'm just telling you why I could not face him. I must forgive him."

"You shouldn't forgive him after what he did!" said Jonathan angrily and Lupus nodded his agreement.

"But I must forgive him."

"Why?"

"Because we are told to love our enemies. Besides, until I forgive him," said Mordecai, tapping his black-robed stomach, "I carry him here, within me. And that is a terrible thing."

Flavia and Nubia wasted their last afternoon in the camp looking for the comic actors Actius and Sorex. Curiously, although many had either seen the play or heard about it, and some had tossed coins to the actors, not one person knew who they were or where they were from.

Jonathan waited until the tent was empty and then went quickly to his father's spare capsa, the cylindrical leather container for medicines and instruments. Quickly he searched through various twists of papyrus, briefly sniffing each one.

Finally he found the one he wanted, untwisted the papyrus and examined the dark brown powder. Yes. He was almost certain this was the one.

Around his neck Jonathan wore a small pouch full of herbs. He opened this pouch and slipped the papyrus twist inside. Then he closed his father's capsa and put it back exactly as he had found it.

"Don't roll your eyes at me like that," he muttered to Ferox. "We're going to an unknown place with a possible criminal mastermind. You never know when you'll need a good sleeping powder!"

■ ■ ■

Flavia saw Pollius Felix return to the camp in the mid-afternoon. He drove a white carruca with gold trim and two white horses, and was followed by a convoy of five carriages, each one loaded with blankets, fig cakes, flour, olive oil, and wine. Each carriage also carried two soldiers who would ensure nothing was stolen, two slaves to help with the physical labor of the distribution, and an imperial scribe to record which provisions went to whom.

Within only an hour the soldiers had erected a large tent near the eastern side of the baths, ready to distribute aid.

"It's too late to start today," said Felix, turning to Gaius. "Will you begin overseeing the operation, Geminus?"

"Of course," replied Flavia's uncle. "I'll be glad of the change to keep myself occupied while my ribs are healing. It won't be strenuous work."

"Excellent," said Felix. "I'll return tomorrow or the next day to see how you're doing and hear any disputes. But now I must return to Surrentum. I believe I am taking your four charges with me." He turned to Flavia. "Are you ready to depart?"

Flavia and her friends nodded. They were clean from an afternoon at the baths. Even the three dogs had been washed and brushed.

"Let's go then." Felix smiled and led the way to his elegant carruca.

They had said their good-byes earlier, and as the carriage drove away from the camp they turned and looked back at Gaius, Miriam, Mordecai, and Aristo. The four figures stood in the road waving, becoming smaller and smaller until the road curved around and they disappeared from sight.

Flavia glanced at her three friends and swallowed. She sensed they were all thinking the same thing.

If Felix was the spider, they were headed straight for his web.

SCROLL X

Flavia was surprised to see Felix at the reins. He had two slaves with him, dark young men no more than twenty years old. But he drove the carruca himself.

And he drove fast.

As soon as it left the camp, the road began to climb the mountainside, twisting and turning. Sometimes they were only a few feet from stomach-churning drops onto the rocks and sea far below.

Flavia sensed it was some kind of test, for every now and then Felix glanced back at them. Each time she returned his smile brightly, though her knuckles hurt from gripping the wooden seat.

Lupus was genuinely enjoying every moment. His eyes blazed with delight at the speed of the carruca. Jonathan, on the other hand, looked rather green. He was trying not to look down on the sea as it foamed against jagged rocks below them.

The dogs lolled on the floor and gave Flavia reproachful looks.

Nubia was not even looking at the sheer drop to their right. She was staring intently at an aqueduct running along the gray mountainside on their left. Flavia followed her gaze. Just before the road curved and the honey-colored cliff blocked her view, she thought she saw three men standing on the top of the aqueduct.

And she was sure one of them had been dark skinned, like Nubia.

They stopped once, after half an hour, so that one of Felix's slaves could relieve himself.

"Stretch your legs," suggested Felix. Handing the reins to the second slave, he jumped down and helped Flavia and the others out of the carruca. Jonathan and the dogs followed the slave behind some oleanders on the other side of the road. Flavia, Nubia, and Lupus walked toward the cliff's edge.

Before them, across the bay, smoldered the remains of Vesuvius. Directly below was a dizzying drop to small coves and the shimmering sea.

Standing there, Flavia realized her legs were trembling. She tried to stop them by stiffening her knees and clenching her fists. She wasn't going to let Felix see she was afraid.

Next thing she knew, he was standing right next to her. His presence was so intense that for a moment everything else seemed unreal. He smiled down at her and took her right hand.

Flavia stared up at him.

"Hold your hand palm down," he said. "That's it. If you curve your forefinger over a little, you have the Bay of Neapolis. See?"

Flavia nodded. His hair smelled faintly of some kind of citron oil.

"The knuckle where your forefinger meets your hand is Vesuvius, or rather what's left of it. . . . No, no. Relax your hand, so the thumb points to your heart. We're here." He touched the web of skin between Flavia's thumb and forefinger. "And we are going to drive along here . . ." Felix moved his well-manicured finger slowly along the inside of Flavia's thumb, ". . . to here, where the pad of your thumb sticks out the most."

He tapped it. "That is the Cape of Surrentum, which some people call the Cape of Hercules. My villa is there."

Felix dropped Flavia's hand and looked with amusement at Lupus, who was hanging his toes over the cliff's edge.

"Lupus," he said. "Would you like to take the reins for a while?"

Lupus turned and stared at him in disbelief. Then, eyes shining, he nodded vigorously.

"Let's go then," said Pollius Felix.

Lupus drove the carriage the rest of the way to Surrentum. At one point the carruca veered so close to the cliff's edge that Flavia screamed and Jonathan began laughing hysterically.

"There's only one thing to do on a road like this," Felix called back to them. "To release the tension you must either sing or shout." He opened his mouth and began to sing a popular song that began *Volare*: "To Fly."

"*Volare!*" sang Felix, as the carriage wheel sent a shower of pebbles skittering into the void, and they all sang with him at the top of their voices.

"*Volare*: To fly! *Cantare*: To sing! To fly in the painted blue sky, to fly so happy and high . . ."

Even Lupus opened his tongueless mouth and yelled out the notes of the song.

After a while they stopped singing, their cheeks wet with tears of laughter.

The song had brought Flavia a strange release. She didn't care if they went hurtling over the edge. She felt immortal, as if she would never die. For the first time since the volcano had erupted she felt totally alive.

As the sun sank lower and lower in the west, Lupus urged the horses along the twisting road through dusty olive groves and orchards. The mountains reared on their left and the cliffs plunged to the sea on their right.

The carriage rattled through Surrentum without stopping and began to climb again. Just as the sun touched the horizon, the horses automatically turned off the main road and trotted down a drive that ran between high stone walls.

Soon the stone wall on their right gave way to columns. Now they were driving beneath a colonnade. The sinking sun painted the white columns orange, and Flavia kept catching glimpses of the shining sea through the twisted ancient olive groves.

The colonnade went on for nearly half a mile, winding down the mountainside toward the sea. The iron-rimmed wheels of the carriage and the horses' hooves resounded in the half-enclosed space.

When at last they emerged into the open, the sudden silence and space around them seemed vast.

The sea blazed like molten copper under the yellow sky of dusk and before them, floating on the water, was the most beautiful villa Flavia had ever seen.

Flavia rubbed her eyes and looked harder. It had been built on an island attached to the mainland by two narrow strips of land. As the carruca stopped and one of the slaves wedged its wheels, Flavia stood up to get a better view. There were columns, domes, fountains, palm trees, and two covered walkways.

A pool of seawater lay between the villa and the mainland, a secret cove, surrounded on all sides by the honey-colored rocks. An arch in the rocks led out to sea, making it a small natural harbor.

As Flavia climbed down from the carruca, a girl about her own age came running from the main complex. She had long golden hair and wore a tunic the same dove-gray as Felix's tunic.

"Pater," she cried with delight, and threw herself into his arms. "Pater! I'm so glad you're home! I was getting terribly worried about you."

"My little nightingale." Felix smoothed a strand of pale gold hair and kissed her forehead. Then he turned to the others.

"This is my eldest daughter, Polla, whom we call Pulchra. Pulchra, meet Flavia Gemina, Jonathan ben Mordecai, and Lupus. Oh, and these are their dogs."

"And this is Nubia. . . ." began Flavia, but Pulchra had gathered Nipur into her arms and was covering his furry black face with kisses.

"Oh, you are so precious!" she gushed. "I just want to eat you up!"

SCROLL XI

"Leda, bring me that box," demanded Polla Pulchra. Then she smiled at Jonathan.

Felix's daughter was showing them her bedroom. It was small, but exquisitely decorated with frescoes of cupids riding dolphins across a dark-blue wall. A window overlooked Vesuvius across the bay, its plume of smoke pink in the evening light.

"Look at that!" said Jonathan, going to the window. "Look at all the ash the volcano is still sending up. . . ."

"I know," sighed Pulchra. "It gets over everything! Leda has to dust twice a day. Leda! My box!"

Pulchra's slave girl, Leda, was a thin pale girl with lank brown hair and dull eyes. She wore a beautiful yellow tunic, but it did not flatter her dingy complexion. She almost stumbled as she held out a small lacquered box to Pulchra.

"Careful!" snapped Pulchra, taking the box impatiently. "These are my jewels," she announced, bringing out various necklaces, bracelets, and bangles for them to admire.

"Nubia has tiger's-eye earrings," said Flavia. "They were given to her by . . . Nubia! One of your earrings is missing!"

"I know," said Nubia. "I lose it in the sand by tent."

Polla Pulchra didn't seem to hear. She had found something.

She set the lacquered box on her bed and turned to Jonathan.

"Look!" She held out a gold ring. "This is a real ruby from Arabia."

"It's . . . um . . . big," commented Jonathan. He wasn't quite sure what she wanted him to say, so he added, "It must be worth a lot of money."

Her pretty face flushed with pleasure. "At least a thousand *sestercii*, according to Pater," she said. "Here. It's yours."

Jonathan stared at her. He'd only met her ten minutes ago and now she had given him a ring worth a fortune.

There was a sudden clatter as the jewelry box slipped from the edge of the bed. Tails wagging, the dogs sniffed the chains and gems on the floor. Pulchra's slave girl stared down in horror.

"You stupid girl!" Pulchra said, and slapped Leda hard across the face. "Pick them up now!"

As the slave girl got down on her hands and knees, Pulchra smiled prettily at Jonathan and gave a little shrug. Then she scooped up Nipur and kissed his nose. "Come on," she said over her shoulder, "we're late for dinner."

"Aren't we going to eat with the rest of your family?" asked Flavia, as Pulchra led them into a small sky-blue dining room with views over the bay.

"No. Pater always has his boring old clients to dinner and Mater usually eats in her rooms. My sisters and I have our own private triclinium."

Pulchra's two younger sisters, Pollina and Pollinilla, were six and five years old, respectively. They had fair hair like Pulchra, though neither was as pretty as their older sister. Each had a slave girl about her own age. After the slaves had washed their dusty feet and given them linen slippers, they reclined.

Pulchra stretched out on her side on the central dining couch and patted the space next to her.

"Recline by me, Jonathan," she said, and as her sisters each took one of the other two couches: "No, you two will have to share a couch so that Fulvia can recline."

"Flavia," said Flavia coldly. "My name is Flavia."

Pulchra looked horrified as Nubia started to lie down beside Flavia.

"Oh, no!" she cried. "You must never let your slave recline at dinner!"

Flustered, Nubia slipped off the couch and hung her head.

"But where will she sit?" asked Flavia.

"You haven't had a personal slave very long, have you?" Pulchra rolled her eyes. "She should stand behind your dining couch like Leda here and cut your food for you!"

Flavia was speechless. But she was a guest and could hardly complain. She gave Nubia a small nod.

Nubia slowly went to stand behind Flavia's couch and Lupus, who had been lingering near the doorway, started to recline beside Flavia.

"No, no!" giggled Pulchra to Jonathan. "*Your* slave should stand behind *you*."

"Lupus isn't a slave, my dear." Pollius Felix stepped into the dining room, smiling at them. It was dusk and he held an oil lamp in one hand.

"Pater! Pater!" The younger girls slipped off their couch and ran to Felix. He put down the lamp, bent to give them each a kiss, and gently directed them back to their couch.

"Oh! But Lupus is so quiet and meek," said Pulchra with a pout. "I was sure he must be Jonathan's slave."

Her father smiled. "Just because he's quiet doesn't mean he's meek." Felix turned to Jonathan. "How is your breathing, now? Are you finding it easier here?"

Jonathan colored a little and coughed. "Um. Yes. It's much better here, sir. Thank you for inviting us."

"Yes," said Flavia, smoothing her hair. "Thank you for inviting us."

Felix turned to Pulchra. "I've come to ask Lupus to dine with us. Can you spare him?"

"Of course," said Pulchra, and caught Jonathan's hand. "But you can't have Jonathan. I want him!"

Pollius Felix led Lupus upstairs to another dining room.

This triclinium looked inward, onto a green inner courtyard. It was twice as big as the dining room Lupus had just left, and the lighting was more subdued. The walls were black, with red panels, and the couches were covered with wine-colored covers and cushions. All the oil lamps were bronze, burnished to a deep gold.

A dozen pairs of dark eyes turned to look warily at Lupus as he stepped into the dining room. The men were reclining or sitting around the room. Lupus guessed their ages ranged from mid-teens to late twenties. Most wore tunics of fashionable sea green and despite the scented oil they used to slick back their hair they exuded a pungent odor of masculinity.

"This is Lupus," said Felix, and Lupus felt the Patron's hand rest lightly on his shoulder. "I sense a rare courage in him. I believe he's as fearless as all of you."

"Pssst! Jonathan! Lupus! Wake up!"

Flavia had waited until the entire villa was silent before creeping next door into Jonathan's room.

"Whuzzit?" mumbled Jonathan and then, "I'm awake. Yes." He yawned, closed his eyes, and snuggled back under the soft woolen cover. It smelled faintly of some disturbingly familiar fragrance.

"Wake up!" hissed Flavia, and shook him again. "We've got to plan tomorrow."

"Mmmph! Oh, all right." Jonathan sat up groggily and pulled the blanket around him. It was after midnight and the air was cool.

Flavia held a small clay oil lamp. She had trimmed the wick so that it burned dimly. Nubia was beside her and so was Lupus, ready with his wax tablet. Jonathan noticed that Lupus's hair was now long enough to be rumpled by sleep. It had been over two months since the barber had shaved it off at the baths in Ostia.

"Why did Felix ask you to dine with him tonight?" asked Flavia.

Lupus crinkled his chin and gave a little shrug.

"Did you learn anything?" asked Jonathan.

Lupus waggled his head to say "not really."

"Who else was there?" said Flavia. "Any pirates?"

Lupus smiled and then took out his wax tablet and stylus. His spelling wasn't perfect, but he could tell them almost anything now, and he relied more and more on writing.

He showed them the tablet:

JUST MEN, XII OR XIII

"Twelve or thirteen men," read Flavia. "Friends?"

Lupus shrugged.

"Slaves?" asked Nubia.

Lupus shook his head.

"Clients?" suggested Jonathan.

Lupus looked at him, narrowed his eyes, and nodded thoughtfully.

"Anyway," said Flavia, "Felix obviously likes you."

Lupus shrugged and looked down.

"Maybe we're mistaken about Felix," said Flavia, brushing a strand of hair away from her face. "He seems to be all right: He knows my uncle, he helped the emperor to bring aid to the camp, and he let Lupus drive the carruca."

"Which proves he's crazy!" Jonathan grinned.

"Crazy, maybe," said Flavia with a blush, "but I like him."

"This is a bad place," said Nubia quietly. "And he is a bad man."

They all looked at her in surprise. Lupus shook his head in angry disagreement.

"Well," said Flavia. "That's what we're here to find out. Lupus, you stick as close to Felix as possible. I think that should be easy. Nubia, you're going to have to stay close to the other slaves and see if you can pick up any gossip from them. I'm sorry Pulchra is treating you so miserably. She's a spoiled, cruel little . . ."

"Hey!" said Jonathan, coloring. "She's not *that* bad."

Flavia started to say something and then changed her mind. "Well, Jonathan, it's obvious that you're the best person to keep an eye on Pulchra. As for me, I'll just generally nose around. We've got to find out as much as we can as quickly as possible, or it may be too late. Any questions?"

They all looked at each other in the dim lamplight.

"I think they divide us," said Nubia quietly.

"Don't be silly," said Flavia with a laugh. "We've been through too much together. But we will have to split up while we're here. We'll lean more that way. We've got to solve this mystery and save the children! Right?"

They all nodded.

SCROLL XII

"Good morning," breathed a soft voice in Jonathan's ear.

Jonathan snuggled deeper into the covers. The blankets were soft and their sweet fragrance was hauntingly familiar. He never wanted to leave.

"Time to get up," whispered the voice and something tickled his ear.

Jonathan opened his eyes a crack and then opened them wide.

Pulchra's face was inches from his. Jonathan immediately sat up, wiped the drool from his chin, and tried to look alert. At the foot of the bed Tigris stretched and yawned.

Pulchra was holding Nipur in her arms and stroking his silky head.

"Look!" she said. "I have a puppy, too!"

"That's Nubia's puppy," he said, and scratched his dark curly hair.

"Don't be silly! Slaves can't own property. They *are* property. Where's Lupus?"

"I don't know."

"Well, Fulvia told me she isn't feeling well today, so you and I can have breakfast all on our own!"

"Oh. Um . . .OK."

Jonathan looked at Pulchra and waited.

Pulchra looked brightly back at Jonathan.

"I'm . . . I'm not wearing any . . . If you could just . . ."

Pulchra giggled. "Oh! You want me to turn around. Very well."

Jonathan quickly got up and slipped on his cream-colored tunic. He noticed someone had cleaned it during the night. It bore the same smell as the blankets.

He splashed his face with water from the jug and reached for a small towel. In the middle of drying his face he stopped and sniffed the towel.

"What is this smell?" he asked Pulchra. "It's in all the blankets and cushions, and now even my tunic smells of it."

"I'll show you!" she caught his hand and pulled him out into the corridor.

It was a still, cool morning just after dawn. A huge moon, almost full and the color of an apricot, floated just above the milky sea.

Jonathan followed Pulchra up some stairs and into an inner garden surrounded by a peristyle. There were ash-dusted jasmine bushes, pomegranates, and quince, but in the middle was a beautiful tree with glossy dark green leaves and heavy yellow fruit. Something about it was different from the other plants around it. He realized what it was.

"It's not covered by ash!"

"Pater had the slaves cover it with a linen cloth soon after Vesuvius erupted," explained Pulchra. "And they dust it every day. It's one of Pater's most precious treasures."

Something stirred deep in Jonathan's memory as he gazed at the tree.

"What kind of tree is it?"

"Some people call it the Persian apple tree but Pater says it's a citron tree. He calls it lemon. He named Villa Limona after this tree. Here," she carefully twisted one of the yellow fruits from the branch and handed it to Jonathan. It was heavy, with a waxy surface, and it filled the palm of his hand.

"Pierce the skin with your fingernail and smell it," she said.

Jonathan dug his thumbnail into the yellow skin and brought the lemon to his nose. Its scent was hauntingly beautiful.

"That lemon alone would cost a hundred sestercii in the markets of Rome," said Pulchra. "We use the oil to preserve wood and we make perfume from the little while blossoms that appear in the spring. We use it for everything. Sniff me." She lifted her golden hair and offered her smooth neck to Jonathan. Tentatively he sniffed the perfumed oil she had dabbed behind her ears.

"Wonderful," he whispered, and for some reason tears sprang to his eyes.

"Pater's dream," said Pulchra, caressing one of the glossy green leaves, "is to cover the hillside with orchards and orchards of these trees."

"And where is your father now?" Jonathan tried to make his voice sound casual.

"Seeing his boring old clients," said Pulchra. "As usual."

"Oh!" said Jonathan, and sniffed the lemon again. "Someone mentioned that your father was quite a powerful man and that even his clients were powerful. They must have been wrong."

Pulchra's blue eyes blazed. "Pater is powerful! More powerful than the emperor himself."

Jonathan shrugged and started to stroll around the garden. "If you say so . . ."

Pulchra caught his hand. Even though there was no one else in sight she brought her lips close to his ear. "I have a secret spying place we can watch him from," she whispered. "Would you like to see it?"

Jonathan turned and looked at her. He had never seen such blue eyes. He nodded.

Lupus made his way carefully down the steep path to the secret harbor. Although the Villa Limona was over twenty miles from

Vesuvius, even here a thin layer of gray ash from the eruption dusted the rocks and wildflowers on either side of the track. He stopped as he realized that the path itself was totally clear of ash. That could mean only one thing: It was frequently used.

He shrugged. Perhaps they just came down to swim. But Felix's daughter had mentioned that they had their own bath complex, so why bathe here? Then he noticed a rowboat pulled up on the shore. It was small, but only a small boat would fit through the arched opening that led to the open sea.

Lupus looked all around. He was alone. Pulling off his tunic, he quickly hid it beneath an oleander bush and stepped into the water. There was a scum of gray ash and pumice dust at the waterline, but farther out the surface of the sea was clean. He slipped naked into the water.

Although its coldness took his breath away, he felt he was home. He had learned to swim before he could walk and now he swam forward with smooth powerful strokes, heading toward the arch in the rocks that led out to sea.

"Shhh! I thought I heard a noise! Is anyone coming?" Flavia was searching Pulchra's bedroom for clues. Nubia stood guard at the door. She peeped out, then turned back and shook her head.

Flavia closed the jewelry box and replaced it on the elegant bronze table. Arranged on the table were the usual things: ivory combs and hairpins, colored glass perfume bottles, a highly polished bronze mirror.

There was also a long thin rod. Flavia frowned and picked it up. It seemed to be made of willow or birch and it tapered at one end. It was slightly sticky. Flavia shrugged and replaced it exactly where she found it.

She turned and surveyed the room. There was a bed with dark blue woolen covers, a bronze standing lamp, and a small leather and bronze stool. There was also a large cedar chest against the wall by the foot of the bed. Flavia tiptoed over to it, undid the latch, and slowly lifted its heavy lid.

She screamed.

Curled up inside the chest was Pulchra's slave girl.

Jonathan squeezed after Pulchra along a narrow space between two walls. They had left the puppies in the garden near the lemon tree and Pulchra had led him through a maze of porticoes and rooms through the kitchen and into a kind of pantry.

"Along here," she gasped, edging her way along. "Pretty soon I won't be able to fit anymore."

A week earlier Jonathan wouldn't have been able to fit either, but he had been in a coma for three days with no food and had eaten very little since. He had never been so thin.

Finally they reached a place with tiny gaps in the bricks. Pulchra silently pointed to one. Jonathan brought his eye close and found he was looking into a large room, a tablinum. He could see the backs of two muscular men in sea green standing beside a column. Beside them stood a short man in a tan tunic. Beyond him Jonathan could see part of a table and a frescoed wall.

After a moment the muscular men shifted to one side and Jonathan saw that Pulchra's father sat behind the table. A scribe in a lemon-yellow tunic stood beside him.

Pollius Felix was leaning back in a bronze and leather chair, listening to the man in the tan tunic. The sun streamed in from the left, illuminating the short man and part of the table, but leaving Felix's face in shadow.

"Please do me this service, Patron," the man in tan was saying. His voice was muffled but perfectly audible. "It's a terrible thing that my lovely little Maia has disappeared. For ten years I have brought you the first crop of olives and the first pressing of oil. I have never asked a favor in return, only your protection. But now I ask that you find her and return her to me and punish the men who took her!"

66

Jonathan and Pulchra exchanged wide-eyed looks, then returned to their peepholes. Felix had risen from his chair and moved out from behind the table. He wore a white toga over a pale blue tunic.

"Rusticus." Felix embraced the man, then held him at arm's length. Jonathan could see the man was a peasant, with sunburned leathery skin.

Felix put an arm around Rusticus and walked him away from the desk, toward Jonathan and Pulchra. "You were right to come to me first, Rusticus. I will find your little Maia and punish the culprits. Tell me what happened."

"My youngest son Quintus saw everything," stammered the farmer. "He and Maia were playing hide-and-seek among the olives when the men appeared." His voice broke. "Maia drew the men away from his hiding place, so that they wouldn't catch him, too."

The farmer stifled a sob and Jonathan saw Felix signal one of his men. A moment later a slave stepped into Jonathan's field of vision with a wine cup.

"Here," said Felix. "Drink this."

The farmer drained the cup and shuddered. "I'm sorry, Patron."

"Don't be ashamed of your tears," said Felix. "A man is never afraid to weep for his family. Tell me. Was there anything else about these men? Anything that might identify them?"

"I'm not sure. My little Quintus has a great imagination, but I don't think he made this up. . . ."

"Go on," said Felix quietly, his arm still around the shorter man's shoulders.

"Quintus said the men who took Maia were wearing masks, like the ones actors wear at the theater. Horrible grinning masks."

SCROLL XIII

Lupus stopped swimming. He rolled over and floated on the gentle swell of the bay, looking back toward the Villa Limona. From most angles it was impossible to see the entrance to the villa's secret harbor.

The villa itself was built on at least four levels. He saw a row of white columns halfway down and realized it was the portico outside his bedroom. On the floor above it, the ground floor, was a large portico. Its columns were fluted and they had red bases.

With all its different levels and domes the Villa Limona looked more like a small village than a villa. Beyond it he could see the long covered colonnade down which he had driven the day before. It was surrounded by silvery-green olives, looking grayer under their covering of ash. Beyond them rose more gray-green slopes, then rugged mountains. The sun was just rising behind them to his left.

Lupus was beginning to get cold, but his short rest had reenergized him so he swam south, away from the villa and its secret harbor.

Some of Felix's slaves were climbing up the rocks on the other side of the villa. He could see their fishing nets full of shining fish thrown over their backs. He stopped to tread water and look.

Near the fishing rocks was a man-made pier. Moored to it was a long sleek ship. It has a mast and sail and holes for ten oars on either side. It was light and narrow, designed more for speed than transport. Beyond it a small headland offered some protection from the winds.

Farther south, the shore became rugged. There was a small beach and then sheer cliffs plunging straight into the water. These cliffs were riddled with grottoes at water level, and caves above.

A flash of color caught Lupus's eye. Emerging from one of the grottoes was a boat. At any other time of day it would have been difficult to see, especially at this distance, but the early morning surface of the water was still milky so the dark blue boat stood out clearly against it.

Flavia and Nubia stared down in horror at the slave girl curled up in the box, and she gazed back, rolling her eyes in terror. She lay on one side with her knees drawn up almost to her face, which was red and swollen from crying.

Flavia couldn't remember the girl's name, but Nubia did. She held out her hand.

"Come out, Leda," she whispered.

Leda shook her head. "I can't," she whimpered. "She'll beat me even more if I don't stay here."

"You mean she knows you're here?" gasped Flavia.

Leda nodded. "She makes me stay in here when I misbehave." The slave girl's nose was running, so Flavia held out a linen hand-kerchief. Leda made no move to take it. She stared as if she had never seen one before.

"It's all right," said Flavia. "Blow your nose. And you can keep it," she added.

"No!" whimpered Leda. "She'd only say I stole it and then she'd beat me."

Flavia and Nubia looked at each other in dismay.

"Please come out," Flavia said. "I'll make sure you aren't punished."

Leda shook her head. "You'll be gone in a day or a week and when you're gone she'll just beat me again, even harder."

Flavia knelt on the floor beside the cedarwood chest so that she wouldn't alarm the slave girl by looming over her.

"Leda," she whispered. "I'll talk to Pulchra. I promise I'll try to make things better for you. Please don't worry." She patted the girl on the shoulder, and Leda winced.

Flavia went cold. She stood and leaned farther over, trying to see the slave girl's back. In one or two places, seeping through the fine yellow linen of her tunic, Flavia could see the dark stain of fresh blood where Pulchra had wielded the birch switch with particular vigor.

Jonathan's stomach growled loudly. For over two hours he'd been riveted to his peephole, watching Felix receive his clients. Now at last, his stomach was protesting. He glanced at Pulchra ruefully. She smiled and nodded and motioned for him to go. But just as he began to edge back toward the kitchen, he felt her hand catch his.

He turned and looked back at her.

Pulchra was pointing urgently toward the peephole.

Curious, Jonathan put his eye back to the chink in the bricks. And gasped.

Felix stood in front of his desk facing left, his fine profile lit by the weak morning sun.

Approaching him was the biggest, ugliest man Jonathan had ever seen. The giant wore a sea-green tunic the size of a ship's sail and his thin black hair was plastered over his balding scalp in ridiculous imitation of the younger men around him. His thighs were so huge that they rubbed together as he moved forward, yet they were not fat, but solid muscle. His chest was massive and his arms muscular and oiled. His nose had been broken at least twice and his ears were swollen like cauliflowers.

The big man lumbered up to Felix, dropped to his knees, and fervently kissed his patron's hand.

Back in the sky-blue triclinium, when it was safe to talk, Jonathan turned to Pulchra. "Who was that huge man?"

"I could tell you some stories about him!" Pulchra dipped a piece of bread in liquid honey and took a dainty bite. "His name is Lucius Brassus and he's one of my father's most loyal soldiers."

Jonathan frowned. "What do you mean soldier?"

"Did I say soldier?" Pulchra giggled. "I meant client of course. . . . Oh, good morning, Fulvia! You're just in time for some breakfast."

Jonathan looked up to see Flavia and Nubia standing in the doorway with Scuto behind them. Flavia's face was pale.

"Oh dear," said Pulchra, "you don't look at all well, Fulvia. And look at your hair! You must ask Leda to arrange it for you right away."

"What's wrong with my hair?" Flavia's hand went automatically to her head.

"Nothing's wrong with it," said Jonathan. "It looks like it always does."

"Oh," said Flavia, and Jonathan was startled by the look of cold fury on her face. Pulchra didn't notice; she was letting Nipur lick honey from her finger.

Jonathan opened his eyes wide at Flavia, as if to say: What's the matter?

She took a deep breath and gave a little shake of her head. Some color returned to her face.

"Actually, Pulchra," said Flavia in a sweet voice, "I'd love Leda to style my hair. You're absolutely right. I can't possibly go out in public with it looking like this. Where is Leda anyway?" Flavia looked around innocently.

Pulchra didn't even bother to look up. "She's in the big cedar chest in my bedroom. Just tell her to do your hair like mine. And you may as well bring her back here afterward."

Lupus had just slipped on his tunic and was pushing his wet hair back from his forehead when he heard voices.

People were coming down the path.

He quickly ducked behind the oleander bushes, grateful that he was wearing his olive-green tunic. He made himself as still and quiet as possible.

"What's her name again?" Lupus heard a man's voice say.

"Maia. Maia Rustica. About nine or ten years old." The second voice was very deep and Lupus thought he recognized it from dinner the night before.

"I don't see why it's so urgent," said the first man. Lupus heard a scraping noise and a splash; they were launching the boat. "Besides, now that she knows where the others are she could ruin everything."

"It's urgent because her father, Rusticus, lives just up the hill," said the man with the deep voice. "He's one of the patron's clients. They never should have taken a child from so close to home. My brother and his friends are idiots. I hear they performed a comedy about pirates on their last night at the refugee camp. Imagine. Risking everything for a few coins!" Deep Voice swore. "Anyway, bring the girl straight back to me."

"I still don't see what good that will do," Lupus heard the first man grumble. There was a creak and the soft plop of oars. He must be in the boat now.

"I'll have a word with her," said Deep Voice. "She's a local girl; she'll know enough to keep her mouth shut."

"All right," said the first man. "I should be back in about an hour."

"I'll be here," said Deep Voice. Suddenly Lupus remembered his name. He was Crispus, a muscular man with black hair, dark stubble on his jaw, and eyelashes as long as a girl's. He'd told a funny joke about two Greek merchants and an olive.

He was also Patron's right-hand man.

SCROLL XIV

Lupus breathed a sigh of relief as he heard Crispus go back up the path. He counted to one hundred and then slowly rose and peered around the dusty oleander. There was no one in sight, so he strolled casually back up the path, as if returning from a morning walk.

His mind was racing. The actors from the camp must be the kidnappers. But who was Maia? How could she ruin everything? And who was Crispus's brother? He needed to talk to Flavia and the others. He turned and passed between marble columns into the garden. It was only three hours past dawn and already the air was shimmering with heat. Then he realized he'd taken a wrong turn. This wasn't the same garden he'd come out of.

He knew his bedroom faced west so he walked away from the rising sun. Yes, there was the sea, straight ahead, visible through more columns. But these columns were fluted, and painted deep red to about his shoulder height. He was on the upper portico, one floor above his bedroom.

He stood and looked out at the view for a moment, enjoying the faint offshore breeze that touched his hair.

"Hello," said a pleasant voice behind him. "Who are you?"

Lupus turned. Sitting in a chair beside one of the columns was a beautiful woman in pale blue. She had delicate features and golden hair.

Lupus flipped open his wax tablet and wrote:

MY NAME IS LUPUS. I CAN'T SPEAK.

"I'm sorry," said the woman, giving him a sweet smile. "Please sit beside me and keep me company for a while." She patted the empty chair next to her.

Lupus hesitated, but only for the briefest moment. Flavia wanted them to learn all they could about Felix. This woman might know something. He sat beside her on a comfortable wicker chair with yellow linen cushions.

"I suppose you're one of my husband's new protégés," the woman said. "He seems to recruit them younger every year. How old are you? About eight?"

Lupus nodded.

She smiled. "My name is Polla Argentaria," she said, "wife of the most powerful man in the Roman Empire. Or so they say. A man who inspires fear or devotion. Sometimes both." She glanced at Lupus. "I can see you are one of those who is devoted to Felix. How does he do that?" she said, almost to herself. "How does he win people's hearts so easily?"

Lupus glanced at her. She had high cheekbones and arched eyebrows.

"I have a theory," said Felix's wife, gazing out toward the horizon. "I believe that when he is with you, he focuses all his power and charm and attention on you alone. The rest of the work seems to fade away and he is yours. But," she said, "at the very moment you think he is yours, you become his."

Lupus looked out toward the horizon, waiting for his face to cool and his heart to stop pounding. When he finally glanced back at her, he saw that she was asleep. He rose carefully, so that the wicker chair would not creak.

As he turned to go, something on the water caught his eye. A small rowboat was moving slowly south, heading for the grottoes.

He must find the others as soon as possible.

Leda climbed out of the cedarwood chest to do Flavia's hair. But before she began, she let the girls smooth balm over the ugly welts on her back.

After that, it took Pulchra's slave girl only a few minutes to arrange Flavia's hair. She pulled it up in an elegant but comfortable twist, held with just four ivory hairpins.

"You're very good!" said Flavia, gazing into Pulchra's bronze hand mirror and patting her hair.

Leda turned bright pink, and Flavia guessed it was probably the first time in her life the slave girl had ever been praised.

Lupus found them all in one of the inner gardens. They were staring at a tree. Apart from the yellow fruit it looked like an ordinary bay tree to him.

As soon as Pulchra's back was turned he signaled Flavia that he had urgent news. Flavia looked pointedly at Pulchra and shrugged, as if to say: What can we do?

". . . and it's worth over a million sestercii," Pulchra was saying.

Lupus saw Flavia looking around for inspiration. Suddenly her eye focused on something on the hillside.

"What's that up in the vineyard?" Flavia asked Pulchra. "It looks like a little temple."

"Oh, that's an ancient shrine to the wine god, Dionysus," said Pulchra importantly. "Of course we own all that land up there."

"Could we go and see it? Dionysus is my favorite god." Lupus had never heard Flavia mention Dionysus before.

"I don't know," said Pulchra slowly. "I don't usually walk anywhere, and it's too steep for a litter. . . ."

"I'd love to go for a walk with you," said Jonathan, with his most charming smile. "I'll bet the view from there is wonderful."

"We could take a picnic lunch," suggested Flavia.

"We want to go! We want to go!" cried Pulchra's little sisters. "A picnic! A picnic!"

"Don't be silly." Pulchra tossed her golden hair. "You're too young. You'd get terribly tired." She turned to the others. "You wait here. I'll tell Cook to prepare a picnic. Come on, Leda!"

Pulchra went off toward the kitchen with her two little sisters clamoring at her heels.

When they were gone the four friends turned to each other and Lupus gave Flavia a thumbs up.

"Quickly," said Flavia. "Before she gets back. Any clues?"

Lupus began to write on his wax tablet.

"Pulchra took me to spy on her own father!" said Jonathan and his dark eyes gleamed. "We watched him receiving his clients for nearly two hours. He gives people money or advice and they kiss his hand and call him Patron and he has one client named Lucius Brassus, who's the size of Ostia's lighthouse. And," Jonathan took a breath and continued before Flavia could comment, "he promised to find the daughter of one of his clients. She was kidnapped yesterday!"

As Jonathan finished speaking, Lupus held his wax tablet behind Jonathan's shoulder.

"Was she by any chance named . . . Maia?" asked Flavia.

Jonathan's jaw dropped. "How did you know?"

Flavia nodded toward Lupus. On his tablet he had written:

MAIA. IX OR X KIDNAPPED.
ARRIVING SOON AT COVE.
I WILL GO AND TRY TO FIND OUT MORE.

Nubia shifted the picnic basket on her shoulder. She and Leda were both carrying baskets and water gourds. The baskets and gourds weren't particularly heavy but Nubia thought the straps must hurt Leda's tender back. Nubia also noted that Leda was barefoot.

Pulchra, on the other hand, wore pretty leather slippers that were totally unsuitable for climbing. Whenever she slipped she squealed and clutched at Jonathan. She soon decided it was easier to hold his hand all the time.

By the time they reached the shrine her pretty yellow locks were clinging damply to her forehead.

"Great Juno!" Pulchra gasped, as they finally reached the small marble building. "Give me that water, Leda."

The dogs had begun by running up the path ahead of them, sniffing eagerly here and there, tails wagging, but they were soon defeated by the heat and humidity. Now they flopped, panting, in the cool shade of an ancient yew tree beside the shrine.

Nubia turned and looked around. She could see for miles. She gazed back down the silver, olive-covered slopes toward the Villa Limona. There were the domes of the bathhouse, the covered walkway, and the spot in the garden where they'd stood an hour before. She could also see the secret harbor. As she watched, a small boat appeared through the arched opening and she saw two figures in it.

Then they were blocked from her view.

Behind her she heard Flavia say, "Can we look inside the shrine?"

Nubia turned.

"I don't think it's locked," Pulchra said, handing the gourd back to Leda without even looking at her.

The temple was made of pink-and-cream marble. Up three steps and through four columns was a bronze door leading into the shrine. Pulchra turned the handle and Jonathan applied his shoulder. The door was heavy but swung open smoothly. They all went in, apart from Leda, who waited outside.

It was a very small shrine, dimly lit by small high windows. The air inside was cool and musty and smelled of stale incense and wine. On the walls were frescoes of dolphins and in front of them was the image of the god: a painted wooden statue of a young man striding forward with an oddly frozen smile. The young god had red lips and black-rimmed eyes that stared over their heads, out toward the blue sea. Around his neck was a withered garland so old it was brown.

"How strange." Flavia was studying the walls. "Why dolphins?"

A movement caught Nubia's eye. A large brown spider moved delicately down the statue's wooden thigh. Nubia shivered and was just turning away when a gleam of gold caught her eye. Something lay on the pedestal near the god's left foot.

While the others were still examining the dolphins on the walls, Nubia quickly reached out and took the tiny object. Her heart was pounding as her fist closed tightly around it.

It was the tiger's-eye earring she had given to Kuanto.

SCROLL XV

As they sat in the shade of the yew tree and unpacked their picnic lunches, Nubia's mind raced.

"What a strange thing to find in a shrine of Dionysus," said Flavia, uncorking her water gourd.

Nubia looked up, alarmed. Had Flavia seen her take the earring?

"Dolphins have nothing to do with the god of wine," mused Flavia. "Satyrs, yes. Or frenzied dancing girls, but dolphins?"

Nubia breathed a sign of relief and bent her head over her lunch again. The cook had prepared six napkins, each wrapped around a selection of delicacies. There were stuffed vine leaves, cold chicken, glossy purple olives, fig cakes, and flat white bread.

As the others were opening their own napkins, Nubia slipped the earring into the leather pouch at her belt. Then she took a bite of chicken and carefully scanned the vines below and the trees above.

Kuanto had told her that when the time was near he would leave her earring where she would see it.

Somehow he had followed and found her. She had spoken to him only once in the refugee camp, was it three nights ago? It had been so dark that she hadn't even been able to see what he looked like. Perhaps he was watching her even now.

Again she studied the trees, looking for the signal. Then she saw it: a scarlet cord tied around a branch of another yew farther up the hill. Nubia forced herself to take another bite of chicken even though her stomach was churning with excitement.

"These stuffed vine leaves are delicious," Flavia was saying to Pulchra. "What's in them?"

"Chickpeas, pepper, and lemon juice," said Pulchra, nipping one neatly in half with her even white teeth and then popping the remaining half into Jonathan's mouth.

"Mmmph!" said Jonathan, then chewed and swallowed. "Tart. But nice."

Flavia was unwrapping hers to examine its contents.

Nubia slowly got to her feet and Flavia squinted up at her. "Are you all right, Nubia? You look . . . strange."

"My stomach is unhappy," said Nubia. "I go behind bushes."

"OK," said Flavia, and turned back to her stuffed grape leaf.

Nubia glanced back once as she walked up toward the yew tree. The others were all intent on their lunches. All except Nipur, who yawned and stretched and trotted after her up the slope, wagging his stubby black tail.

Lupus watched from the hillside above the Villa Limona as the girl stepped out of the rowboat onto the shore of the secret cove.

Crispus was waiting for her, looking around nervously. When she reached him he bent down and spoke to her urgently. The girl was crying, but she nodded her head. Finally Crispus stood and tousled her dark hair.

Then he took the girl's hand and led her up the path. They went into the stables, and a moment later emerged on horseback, with the girl sitting in front of Crispus. Lupus hadn't expected that.

As they trotted past him, he hid behind an ancient olive tree, then slipped off his sandals and ran after them. The white paving stones were smooth on his bare feet, for the covered drive was as superbly made as any Roman road, gently rising in the middle and with drains to carry away rainwater on either side. It occurred to him, as he ran, that only a cohort of legionaries could have built such a road. He wondered how Felix had arranged it and how much it cost.

By the time he'd reached the main coastal road his heart was pounding and he was gasping for breath. Lupus looked right and left and up the slopes. But the horse and its riders were nowhere to be seen.

Nubia reached up and touched the scarlet cord.

The trunk of the yew screened her from the others and she looked eagerly around for another red cord. There it was! Tied around the lowest branch of a tree farther up the slope. She ran to it as lightly and quickly as she could, conscious that the others would soon wonder where she was.

Nipur growled at a movement in the shrubbery. Before she could gasp, someone grabbed her around the waist and a hand covered her mouth. She felt hot breath in her ear and heard a voice whisper, "It's me. Fuscus. Kuanto, I mean. Don't scream."

He released her slowly and Nubia turned to look at him.

Kuanto of the Jackal Clan stood looking down at her. She guessed he was the age of her eldest brother, about sixteen or seventeen. He was smiling at her with perfect teeth and she felt her face grow hot.

He was very handsome.

Later that afternoon, Nubia stood behind Flavia combing her mistress's light brown hair, still damp from the baths.

"Do you think you can do my hair the way Leda did it this morning?" asked Flavia. Her gray eyes were sparkling. They'd been invited to dine with Pollius Felix and his wife.

Pulchra's sisters had run to meet them as soon as they got back from their picnic.

"Pater and Mater have invited us to dine with them tonight," they squealed with excitement. "All of us."

"Don't be silly," Pulchra had replied irritably; she was very hot and tired. But it had been true.

"This is a real honor," Pulchra told Flavia at least half a dozen times while they made the circuit of the Villa Limona's private baths. "They almost never dine with us anymore." And Nubia had noticed a strange expression on Pulchra's face.

After their bath, Nubia tried to arrange Flavia's hair the way Leda had done it that morning.

"Thank you, Nubia." Flavia patted her hair and looked in the bronze mirror. "You've done it just as nicely as Leda did it. I can't believe Felix is actually going to dine with us. . . ." She sighed. "Now where's my bulla?"

Nubia bent to do the fine clasp of the silver chain around Flavia's neck. Attached to the chain was a bulla—the charm worn by free-born children until they were considered grown up. As Nubia tried to open the clasp, she wondered if anyone would ever comb her hair again, as her mother used to do. Her fingers were still oily from rubbing Flavia down and the chain slipped and the bulla fell onto the tiled floor.

"Stupid!" muttered Flavia angrily. She bent to retrieve it and thrust it impatiently at Nubia. With shaking hands, Nubia finally managed to do the clasp.

"Do I look all right?" said Flavia, holding up the bronze mirror again.

But Nubia could tell she wasn't expecting an answer.

As Flavia followed Pulchra into the private triclinium of Polla Argentaria, she was handed a garland of ivy, miniature yellow roses, and lemon leaves. Pulchra's younger sisters were already there, reclining on cream linen couches. So were Jonathan and Lupus. They both wore new sea-green tunics. Lupus had slicked his dark hair back from his forehead.

"Very fashionable!" observed Flavia.

Lupus tried to look unconcerned as he adjusted his garland, but Jonathan colored. "I think they're a gift from Felix. They were laid out on our beds when we came out of the baths."

Nubia was already there, standing beside Leda. She wore one of the lemon-yellow tunics worn by all the slaves of the Villa Limona. The color glowed against her dark skin and Flavia was proud to have such a beautiful slave girl standing behind her as she reclined.

The walls of the north-facing dining room were pale yellow, with an elegant black-and-cream frieze of winged cupids riding chariots. In one corner of the room was a Greek sculpture of Venus; the bronze goddess was shown undressing for her bath. Beneath the statue of Venus sat a young slave strumming melodious chords on a lyre. It was definitely a woman's dining room, decided Flavia. She could hardly wait to see what Felix's wife looked like.

At last, followed by their slaves, Publius Pollius Felix and his wife Polla Argentaria stepped into the dining room.

SCROLL XVI

Polla was almost as tall as her husband, and very beautiful. But it was a pale, transparent beauty, and she seemed almost ghostlike beside Felix's intense presence.

After the introductions had been made, Felix and Polla reclined on the central couch. The serving girls immediately brought in the first tables and set them before the couches.

The first course consisted of hard-boiled quail eggs and button mushrooms glazed with honey and fish sauce. They were delicious, and small enough to be eaten elegantly. Lupus seemed to like them, probably because they slipped down his throat so easily.

As they ate, Felix turned to Flavia, who reclined on the couch to his right. "Tell me, Flavia Gemina," he said, "what did you do today?"

For a moment Flavia was tempted to say, "We spied on you," but instead she said, "We walked up to the shrine of Dionysus and had a picnic lunch there."

"The wine god loves the hills, the north wind, and the cool shade of the yew tree," quoted Felix.

"Virgil?" asked Flavia.

Felix opened his eyes in surprise and nodded. "*The Georgics*. I'm impressed."

"Why are dolphins painted on the walls of his shrine?" asked Flavia, not wanting to lose his attention.

Felix raised one of his dark eyebrows and gave her an amused glance. "I'm surprised a well-educated girl like you doesn't know the connection." He glanced up and whispered something to the slave who stood behind him. The young man nodded and hurried out of the dining room.

A moment later the slave was back. He handed Felix a ceramic drinking cup and resumed his place behind his master's couch.

Felix held the cup out to Flavia. She could tell at once that it was Greek and probably an antique, so she took it carefully with both hands.

"It's an Athenian kylix," said Felix, "one of the most valuable antiques I own. Any idea how old it is?"

Flavia thought quickly. Her uncle Gaius had a mixing bowl with red figures on black that was over five hundred years old. This elegant cup had black figures on red, and she knew black-figure was even older than red-figure.

"Over six hundred years old?" she hazarded a guess.

Felix raised both eyebrows this time. "Again I'm impressed, Flavia Gemina. Very impressed. Now, can you tell me who is painted inside?"

Painted in black glaze on the bottom of the cup's wide flat bowl was an elegant ship with a white sail and a tiny white dolphin on its prow. The potter had painted a man reclining in the ship, completely filling it up. This figure wore a garland on his head and in his hand he held a wine cup.

Flavia studied the kylix for a moment and then held it up so that Pulchra, Jonanthan, and Lupus could see, too.

"It's Dionysus, the god of wine, isn't it?" said Pulchra.

"Clever girl," said Felix with a smile. "But tell me, what's unusual about the scene?"

"The fact that there's an enormous grapevine growing up the mast?" suggested Jonathan.

"Exactly."

"And there are six, no—seven dolphins swimming in the water," said Flavia.

"The Greek poet Homer tells the story in his seventh hymn," said Felix, as the serving girls cleared away the tables.

"One day the god Dionysus was standing on the shore of the Tyrrhenian Sea, when some pirates came sailing by. Even from a distance they could see he was a nobleman so they decided to kidnap him and ask an enormous ransom."

Flavia, Jonathan, and Lupus exchanged glances.

"The pirates dragged the god into their ship and tied him up. But when they were well out to sea, Dionysus caused the ropes that bound him to become grapevines. The vines curled up the mast and over the rigging and in no time bore huge clusters of blue-black grapes. The pirates gazed at each other in horror. They knew their captive must be a god, one of the immortals."

Felix was reclining with a garland on his head as he told the story, and Flavia could easily imagine what Dionysus had looked like.

"Suddenly," said Felix, "Dionysus turned into a lion and roared in their faces. After all, he is the god of wine, intoxication, and madness. The pirates leaped overboard before the beast could devour them."

Lupus guffawed loudly and Felix gave him an amused glance.

"Then the god became himself again and enjoyed a leisurely cup of wine as the boat carried him back home."

"But what do the dolphins have to do with the story?" asked Flavia.

"Well," said Felix, "the wine put Dionysus in such good spirits that he took pity on the drowning sailors and turned them all into dolphins. And that is how dolphins came to be."

"What a wonderful story," sighed Flavia, gazing at the brave and handsome god who vanquished pirates. At last she handed the beautiful cup back to Felix.

He gave a little shake of his head. "Keep it," he said. "It's yours."

Flavia felt her face go cold and then hot. She swallowed and tried to protest. But no words came.

Felix smiled. "What good are riches if you can't give them away?" he said. "Friends are far more important than possessions."

The serving girls brought in the second course: whitefish, baked fennel, and sweet baby onions. The fish was cod, baked in a crust of rock salt and coriander seeds. Beside each piece was a wedge of lemon.

"Finally! Some lemon!" cried Jonathan. He popped the entire wedge into his mouth and began to chew it.

At the look on his face everyone burst out laughing, especially Pollina and Pollinilla, who screamed with laughter and kicked their chubby legs in the air. Polla smiled and made a subtle gesture. Her slave demonstrated how to squeeze the lemon wedge over the fish.

Jonathan squeezed another wedge of lemon over his fish and tentatively took a bite. It was salty and sour at the same time. And absolutely delicious.

"Speaking of Dionysus . . ." said Felix, and nodded at a slave hovering in the doorway. The wine steward moved smoothly forward, a jug in either hand. Expertly he filled each guest's cup, simultaneously pouring out foamy black wine from one jug and clear water from the other. The mixture ranged from ruby red in Felix's cup to palest pink for the little girls.

Felix took a sip of wine and closed his eyes to fully savor the taste. Then he raised his cup to Flavia.

"Your uncle's wine," he said, "the finest wine in the region. What a pity his vineyards are now buried under the ash of Vesuvius."

"Did you see the ash when you took the emperor back to Stabia?" asked Jonathan.

"Indeed I did," said Felix. "There were treasure hunters trying to tunnel their way into rich men's houses."

"Did they find anything?" asked Jonathan. Lupus, reclining next to him, sat up on his elbow with interest.

"Only their own graves. The ash has hardened on top, but it's only a crust. If you walk on the crust you fall in. Then you sink down and drown in the ash."

Jonathan shuddered.

"So far," continued Felix, "despite what Titus said, we have not found one person alive. I don't think you realize how lucky you were to survive. The gods must surely have favored you." He sipped his wine and turned his dark eyes on Flavia.

"Tell us, Flavia Gemina, how did you manage to escape the volcano?"

Flavia told them.

When she started her story, the evening sky was as pink as half-watered wine, and a slave was lighting the bronze lamps. When she finished, night had fallen. One or two of the brighter stars winked dimly above the horizon.

Flavia looked up and realized the lyre player had stopped strumming some time ago; he was staring at her, his mouth wide open. The serving girls stood transfixed in the doorway, unwilling to take out the main course and miss any of the tale. Polla had a pained look on her face, as if she had experienced the terror of that night with them.

And Flavia knew without looking that Felix's eyes had never left her face. She glanced at him quickly and felt a thrill of pleasure at the admiration in his eyes.

"Remarkable," he murmured. "I think we should celebrate your survival with something special. Pulchra? Do you agree?"

"Yes, Pater!" she clapped her hands. "The lemon wine!"

Pollina and Pollinilla had been dozing off. But now they were wide awake, chanting: "Lemon wine! Lemon wine!"

Felix nodded at the wine steward, who tried to suppress a smile.

The serving girls took away the empty plates and brought dessert: honey-soaked sesame cakes.

"Mmmm, my favorite," said Jonathan, licking the honey from his fingers.

The wine steward appeared with a painted wooden tray. On it were a dozen small cups of fine Alexandrian glass. Flavia knew they were of the highest quality because the glass was almost clear. In the center of the tray was a clear glass decanter full of bright yellow liquid.

The steward filled the little glasses and gave one to each of the guests.

Flavia sipped hers. It was tart and lemony, but at the same time deliciously sweet and sticky. She drained it and boldly extended her empty glass for a refill.

Felix was tuning the strings of a lyre. "My turn to tell a story," he said. "Or rather, to sing a story."

For a while he played a complicated bittersweet tune. Then he began to sing. Pollina and Pollinilla had fallen asleep, their faces flushed and damp, their fine hair golden in the lamplight. Pulchra gazed at her father with adoration. Lupus was watching him, too, his eyes as green and still as a cat's. Polla's eyes were closed, but she was not asleep.

Felix sang a song Flavia was not familiar with. It was a song about the Cretan princess Ariadne, and how she found love on the island of Naxos. His voice was slightly husky and he sang as beautifully as he played. When he finished everyone applauded, but softly, so as not to wake the little girls.

Polla opened her eyes, "My husband is too modest to tell you," she said quietly, "but he wrote the song himself and won a prize for it at the festival last year."

Felix inclined his head graciously. Then he turned to Flavia. "Do you play?"

Flavia's heart sank. The only instrument she could play was the tambourine, and even that not very well. Then she had an idea.

"I don't play, but Nubia does!" she glanced over her shoulder. "Nubia, play your flute for us! Come on!" Flavia tugged the hem of Nubia's yellow tunic in order to pull her onto the foot of the dining couch.

Nubia was not used to standing for so long and she was glad to sit. As she took out her flute she was aware of everyone watching her, so she closed her eyes to concentrate. After a moment a picture came into her mind.

She lifted the flute to her lips and began to play. She played a new song, a song her father had never taught her, a song her brother had never taught her. In her mind Nubia called it "Slave Song."

She played the desert at sunset, with slanting purple shadows, and a line of swaying camels, moving on, always on.

Riding one of the camels was a girl whose amber eyes were full of tears. The girl had nothing. Her family was gone. Her tents were burned. Her dog lay in the dust. The girl's back was raw from the whip, and around her neck was a cold iron collar.

But the tears on her cheek were tears of joy.

A crescent moon hung above the horizon. Beneath it were date palms, silhouetted against a violet sky. An oasis.

She knew there would be water there. And honey-sweet dates. And cool silver sand. And someone who cared for her.

And best of all, freedom.

Flavia woke the next morning with a throbbing headache and a sick feeling in the pit of her stomach. She didn't even remember going to bed.

"Nubia?" she croaked. "Bring me some water, please. My throat feels as dry as ash. Nubia?" She could tell from the heat and the brightness of the sunlight that it was very late, probably mid-morning.

She groaned, sat up in bed, and looked around blearily. The dogs were not there and Nubia was gone, too. Grumpily, Flavia slipped on her tunic and sandals and rose unsteadily to her feet.

Then she sat down again, because she felt dizzy. There was a jug and beaker beside her bed, so she filled the beaker with water and drank it down.

She stood up and took a step forward.

Then she sat down again, this time because she felt sick.

On the floor near Nubia's bed were drops of blood. And next to them lay Nubia's lotus-wood flute, broken in half.

SCROLL XVII

"Where is she?" said Flavia quietly, trying to keep her voice from shaking.

"Oh, good morning, Fulvia," said Pulchra. "Or should I say, good afternoon?" Pulchra was sitting with Jonathan on her bed. They were playing a board game.

"Where's who?" said Jonathan absently, trying to decide his next move.

"Nubia. She's missing. I've been looking everywhere for her. And her lotus-wood flute is broken."

"I haven't seen her today." Jonathan put down his counter and looked at Flavia. "I thought she was still asleep in your room."

"No. She isn't." Flavia folder her arms and stared at Pulchra, who was studying the board.

"Pulchra?" said Flavia at last. "Where is Nubia?"

"She was insolent," said Pulchra, without looking up. "I only wanted to look at her flute and she wouldn't even let me touch it. She ran off and I assumed she went crying back to you. You're far too soft on her, you know. She's terribly spoiled."

"What did you do to her?"

"I beat her, of course." Pulchra's blue eyes flickered nervously up at Jonathan.

"And?" Flavia's lips were white with fury.

"And I broke her silly flute."

"I know Felix will help us," said Flavia to Jonathan an hour later.

They stood in the garden in the cool shade of the lemon tree. When Jonathan had seen the look of fury on Flavia's face he had scrambled off the bed and hurried her out of Pulchra's room. Pulchra hadn't the nerve to follow them. The two of them had searched the Villa Limona for nearly an hour before they found a slave who claimed he had seen a dark-skinned girl going up the mountainside.

"Felix found that other girl," Flavia continued feverishly. "He has lots of men and servants. We don't know the hills around here but his men do. He'll help us find Nubia before something happens to her. I know he will."

"I'm not sure," said Jonathan doubtfully.

"Of course he will. Come on. I'll prove it to you."

It was almost midday and Felix had seen all but a few of his clients. There were only two other men still waiting when they stepped into the atrium.

Felix's secretary raised an eyebrow when they told him they wanted to see the patron, but Flavia assured him that she was a client, so he noted her name on his wax tablet.

She flopped on the cold marble bench beside Jonathan and looked around the atrium outside Felix's study. It was cool but light, lit by the usual rectangular gap in the high ceiling.

"Oh, Jonathan," she sighed. "Why didn't Nubia come straight to me after Pulchra beat her?"

"Well . . ." Jonathan began, and then hesitated.

"What?" Flavia scowled at Jonathan. She was still feeling sick from too much lemon wine.

"You've started treating Nubia the same way Pulchra treats Leda."

"Don't be ridiculous."

"Last night at dinner she stood behind your couch all evening and she didn't have a bite to eat and then you commanded her to play her flute, just so you could impress that spider. . . ."

"That what?" Flavia knew he meant Felix.

Jonathan looked at her. "Remember at the camp, the innkeeper telling us about the spider and the web? Well I think Felix is a big fat spider."

The double doors of Felix's study opened and they heard voices from inside.

"Thank you, Patron, thank you. I don't know how I can ever repay you. You are like one of the gods, bringing my little girl back to me from the dead."

A short peasant in a tan tunic backed out of the tablinum, his arm around a dark-haired girl. As they turned to go, Flavia saw he was smiling through tears of joy.

"Some spider!" she snorted.

The secretary came out and murmured apologetically to the two men waiting on the other side of the atrium. Then he approached Flavia and Jonathan.

"The patron will see you now."

"Flavia. Jonathan. Come in."

Behind his table, Felix stood to greet them. He wore a toga over his tunic and Jonathan thought it made him seem even more impressive than usual.

"Sit and tell me what I can do for you," said Felix. He gestured to two chairs on the other side of his table. As Jonathan moved to sit, he glanced quickly at the back wall, wondering whether the peepholes were visible.

The plaster-covered wall was pale blue, with rectangular panels of deep red. On the panels were frescoes of comic and tragic masks, skillfully painted so that they seemed to really hang from the wall. The plaster had slight cracks in places, but this gave the frescoes an impressive antique appearance.

Jonathan couldn't see the spy holes anywhere, but he noticed a dark-haired boy in a sea-green tunic leaning against a column. Flavia saw him at the same moment.

"Lupus!" she cried.

Lupus gave them a small nod, but did not smile. He turned his gaze back toward Felix.

Flavia sat and faced Publius Pollius Felix. "Patron," she said, getting straight to the point, "we need your help."

Felix had taken a seat on the other side of his desk. "How can I help you, Flavia Gemina?" His tone was cool.

"Nubia is missing. Please can you find her?"

Felix frowned. "Who's Nubia?"

"My slave girl," said Flavia, and Jonathan could see she was surprised he didn't know.

"Ah, the dark-skinned girl who played last night. A curious tune, neither Greek nor Roman. You say she's missing?"

"She ran away this morning, after . . ." Flavia stopped and began again. "I think she ran away."

"Flavia Gemina," said Felix, "I do have men who track down runaway slaves, but I must tell you that when we find these slaves we punish them according to Roman law. I suggest you wait until she returns of her own accord. Meanwhile, please feel free to take any female slave you like from my household as a replacement. Just check with Justus here that it's one who is dispensable." He glanced up at his scribe, who nodded and made a note.

"But Nubia might be in danger!"

Felix leaned forward onto his desk and gave Flavia a sympathetic look that Jonathan didn't trust one bit.

"I can see you're very fond of her," said Felix quietly. "But the emperor has just decreed that runaway slaves should be crucified or executed in the amphitheater. If my men find her . . ."

Jonathan shivered and glanced at Flavia, who had turned as white as Felix's toga.

"I'm sorry," continued Pollis Felix, "but we don't want another slave revolt and that's how we maintain control. It's especially important now, after the volcano has caused so much chaos. We've heard many reports of damage and theft caused by runaway slaves."

"But she's my friend," said Flavia. "She saved my life."

"You love your dog, too, I imagine," he said. "But if he were rabid you would have to put him down, wouldn't you?" Felix sat back and opened his hands, palms to the ceiling. "I'm sorry, Flavia. In this case I'm afraid I must refuse your request."

SCROLL XVIII

"You were right, Jonathan," sobbed Flavia. "He's a big fat spider."

They had barely left the atrium before Flavia burst into tears. She slumped beneath the shade of the lemon tree. Jonathan sat beside her and patted her shoulder.

"And Nubia was right, too." She turned her blotched face toward Jonathan, "He's divided us. He makes you love him and then . . . Lupus is under his spell, too."

Hot tears splashed onto her knees and tunic, and her whole boy shuddered with sobs. Jonathan tried to console her by patting her back. Scuto wandered into the garden and came up to his mistress, wagging his tail.

Flavia threw her arms around his woolly neck and sobbed into his fur. Scuto sat, panting gently and rolling his eyes at Jonathan.

A shadow fell across them and they looked up.

It was Lupus. The sun was behind his head so they couldn't see the expression on his face. But his feelings were made clear by the wax tablet he held out. On it he had written:

WHAT ARE YOU WAITING FOR?
LET'S FIND NUBIA OURSELVES!

■■■

Flavia took Scuto's big head between her hands and gazed into his brown eyes. "Find Nubia, Scuto. Nu-bi-a." She let him sniff the lemon-yellow tunic Nubia had worn the night before. "Go on, Scuto. You, too, Tigris." She stood up. "Go find her!"

As the three friends followed Scuto and Tigris up through the silver olive groves, Flavia cast her mind back over the events of the previous day.

She thought about the beautiful song Nubia had played the night before, of the yearning it had expressed. She remembered how she had muttered "stupid" while Nubia was helping her dress for dinner and a terrible thought occurred to her. She'd been thinking about Felix and how wearing a bulla was stupid, because it showed she was still just a little girl. But perhaps Nubia had thought she'd meant it for her.

And later, at dinner, she had been so busy trying to impress Felix that she hadn't even looked at Nubia, standing patiently behind her. She assumed the slaves would eat, too, but of course they hadn't had a chance. They probably fought for scraps in the kitchens afterward.

Flavia stopped and uncorked her water gourd. She felt sick from the heat and too much lemon wine. After a long drink she continued up the path after the boys.

It was all Pulchra's fault, thought Flavia, grinding her teeth. That stupid, spoiled little harpy with her golden hair and her big blue eyes. She had dared to strike Nubia! And then she had broken Nubia's precious flute!

Flavia's anger gave her strength and before she knew it she was standing at the shrine of Dionysus while the dogs sniffed excitedly around the yew tree.

Flavia's heart sank.

"Oh, no'" she said to the boys, and her eyes filled with tears of frustration. "They haven't followed her scent from today. They followed it from yesterday!"

■■■

"Wait!" said Jonathan. "Tigris is going farther up the hill. We didn't go that far yesterday." Now Scuto had the scent, too, and was following Tigris into a grove of pine and yew trees.

"Nubia had to relieve herself," said Flavia, not bothering to look.

"Are you sure? All the way up there?"

Flavia turned and peered through the dappled shade up the hill. Lupus grunted and pointed.

"What?" said Flavia. "Do you see something?"

"A red cord!" cried Jonathan. "Tied to that branch."

"Yes, I see it! And there's another farther up! They look like markers for a trail. Let's follow them!"

The red cords led them up the hill, across a road, and over a low ridge. Now they were out of sight of the Villa Limona. Jonathan was wheezing a little, so they stopped in a clearing and looked out at the new vista that lay before them.

The sea shimmered in a heat haze beneath the noonday sun. Below them a silvery blanket of olive groves rolled down to the shore. On the slopes rising behind them the pines thinned and eventually gave way to rugged cliffs honeycombed with caves.

Scuto stood for a moment, eyes half closed, testing the wind with his nose. Tigris was already moving farther up the path, so intent on tracking Nipur's scent that he only wagged his tail occasionally.

"Look, there's an island out there," Flavia pointed. "I wonder if that's Caprea."

Jonathan stood very still.

He knew this place. And yet he had never been here in his life. He stared at the distant island and the sea. From this height, the water looked like dark blue silk. He almost remembered. Then the memory slipped away, like smoke.

Behind him a twig snapped and there was the faint rustle of leaves.

"Flavia! Lupus!" he hissed. "Someone's following us!"

■■■

Flavia heard it the moment Jonathan did: Someone was coming up the track behind them. Lupus put his finger to his lips and melted into the shade of the pine trees.

A moment later he was back, tugging a very pink-faced Pulchra by the wrist. Leda trailed behind him.

"You!" cried Flavia, stalking forward and thrusting her face close to Pulchra's. "Why are you following us? Haven't you caused enough trouble already?"

Pulchra took a small step backward. "We weren't following you. We were just going for a walk."

"Dressed in those old green tunics? You were too following us!"

Pulchra tried to toss her hair but it stuck damply to her neck.

"I thought you might need some help," she said imperiously, folding her arms.

"What? Help us find Nubia so your father can have her crucified? You . . . you spoiled little patrician!"

"Peasant!" retorted Pulchra, narrowing her eyes.

"Harpy!"

"Gorgon!"

Furiously, Flavia grabbed a handful of Pulchra's yellow hair and tugged as hard as she could. "You should be whipped yourself!" she yelled.

Pulchra screeched and aimed a few feeble blows at Flavia.

"You fight like a girl!" sneered Flavia, easily fending them off.

"I am . . . a girl . . ." gasped Pulchra, "unlike YOU!" She punched Flavia hard in the stomach.

Flavia doubled over, trying desperately not to be sick, then furiously tackled Pulchra around the knees and brought her thudding down onto the dusty ground.

"Oof!" cried Pulchra.

Flavia straddled her but Pulchra writhed and twisted furiously.

Lupus, Jonathan, and Leda watched in stunned amazement as the two girls rolled on the ground.

"Ow!" yelled Flavia, as Pulchra sunk her perfect white teeth into Flavia's forearm. "Biting's not fair!" And she raked her fingernails hard across Pulchra's cheek and neck.

Pulchra screamed and thrashed with her legs and arms.

Lupus and Jonathan moved forward to separate them, but the girls weren't holding back now and the boys hesitated over the tumbling pair.

Somewhere up the hill, Scuto barked his warning bark, but they didn't hear him. And they didn't see the masked men come out of the bushes until it was too late.

SCROLL XIX

There were only two of them, but they were strong men, hardened by rough living and scouring the mountains for stray children.

Lupus was the only one who got away.

Jonathan fought back, but was still weak from his recent coma. A blow to his head left him stunned and sick on the ground. Leda simply stood there and allowed them to tie her hands. Flavia and Pulchra were still rolling in the dust when the masked men lifted them apart and wrenched their hands behind their backs. When she saw the leering masks, Pulchra screamed.

"Pollux!" cursed Flavia, and kicked out at the little one. But she was exhausted from fighting Pulchra and her foot failed to connect.

Within moments, the four of them stood in the hot sunshine, their hands bound tightly behind their backs. Flavia and Pulchra were still breathing hard, covered with dust and blood.

Scuto stood at the edge of the clearing, half wagging his tail. He was not sure whether it was a game.

"Well, Actius," said the short one from behind his grinning mask, "this is the best haul we've had so far."

"It certainly is, Sorex, it certainly is," said the tall one, who also wore a mask. "Two lively ones and two not-so-lively ones."

"One got away."

"Yes. Pity about that one. But he was smaller. You have to throw the small ones back sometimes. Anyway, four brings the total up to fifty. A nice round number."

"A very nice round number," agreed Sorex. "Lucrio says the patron promised another ten thousand sestercii if we could get our numbers up to fifty."

The patron.

Watching and listening from the bushes, Lupus couldn't believe what he had heard. He felt sick. Could Felix really be behind this?

No, there must be some mistake. They couldn't be Felix's men. It must be another patron they meant. Surely if Felix was their patron they would recognize his daughter, Pulchra.

Besides, Felix used his power to help his clients, not hurt them. He had helped the farmer find his daughter and he had loaned the tent maker money to help him expand his business. Lupus knew that Felix had personally paid for many of the provisions for the refugee camp.

He shifted to get a better view. The masked men were shoving his friends, prodding them across the clearing. Scuto stood nearby, his tail wagging hesitantly. Suddenly a black puppy raced down the hillside and sunk his teeth into the shorter man's ankle. Unlike Scuto, Tigris knew the men were not playing a game.

The masked man cursed and kicked the puppy hard. Tigris flew up into the air, then landed in the dust with a thud. He lay motionless.

"Tigris!" Lupus saw Jonathan twist to look back. But the masked men laughed and pushed him roughly toward a rocky path that led down the mountain to the sea.

SCROLL XX

Jonathan needed all his powers of concentration to descend the path, but that was good. Anything that took his mind off the image of Tigris lying so still in the dust was good. So he focused on putting one foot in front of the other. Going downhill was always harder than going uphill, because it was so easy to slip. And with his hands tied behind his back it was almost impossible to keep his balance.

Twice already Pulchra had slipped and skidded on her bottom down the path. The masked men had laughed before yanking her roughly to her feet. She had been sobbing ever since

Jonathan started to slip, too. He only just caught himself, but in doing so he wrenched his ankle and it hurt so much that tears sprang to his eyes.

"Oh, dear!" said Sorex, who had an oddly high voice. "We almost lost Curlytop."

"Do you think we should untie their hands?" said Actius. He was the tall one with the deeper voice.

"And spoil all our fun?" squeaked Sorex. "Not on your life. I wager two sestercii that Blondie's going to fall at least once more before we reach the Green Grotto."

"You're on."

■■■

Lupus knelt beside Tigris and put one ear against the puppy's chest. Tigris was very still, but he was still warm, and Lupus could hear his little heart beating. Scuto whined softly.

Lupus gathered the puppy into his arms and stood.

For a while he and Scuto followed the track down the mountain, but Tigris was a big puppy and Lupus's arm soon grew tired. He stopped. He reckoned the men could only be going one place. To the grotto from which he'd seen the boat emerging the day before. It must be their hideout.

Lupus didn't need to go any farther. He needed to get Tigris back to the Villa Limona. And then he needed to get help.

He would go to Felix. Despite what the masked men had said, he felt sure the patron had nothing to do with the kidnappings. He knew Felix wouldn't let him down.

At last Flavia and the others reached level ground. They were on the cliffs above the sea. The masked men were prodding them toward a small pomegranate tree between them and the cliff's edge. It was only when they were nearly upon it that Flavia saw a depression in the ground with steps leading down. The masked men untied their hands.

"Down you go," said Sorex, the small one. His eyes behind the grinning mask were cold. "Don't try anything or you'll go head-first."

Flavia started down the steps, followed by Pulchra, Jonathan, and Leda. Their captors took up the rear.

The stairs descended into darkness. As the weak white light of the overcast sun grew fainter behind her, Flavia moved carefully, feeling her way with her feet, fingertips touching damp rock on either side. Gradually the steps curved to the left and then Flavia emerged into a huge cool blue-green space.

It was a grotto.

"Move along!" Sorex's nasal voice echoed strangely in the vast space. Flavia found herself standing on a broad shelf of rock. Before her, a pool of milky blue water filled the dome of the cave with a bluish-green light. Above Flavia's head, the ceiling was ridged and arched, like the roof of Scuto's mouth when he yawned. Somewhere water dripped, echoing eerily in the vast enclosed space. Bright daylight streamed in to her right. Flavia knew that must be the way out to the sea.

She was just wondering whether she should risk jumping in the water and trying to swim away when the one called Actius tied her hands behind her back again.

The kidnappers had removed their masks before coming down the dangerous steps and now Flavia saw their faces. Sorex had a small red mouth, a snub nose, and a cleft chin. Actius had a large head and big smooth features.

Flavia heard footsteps and saw a third man approaching from the left. His face, lit green by the shimmering water, looked familiar. It was the announcer from the refugee camp, the man who had introduced the two actors.

"Hey, Lucrio. Look what we found wandering the hills." Sorex's high voice echoed in the vast space of the Green Grotto.

"Well, well, well!" said Lucrio. He had a narrow face and cheeks dark with stubble. "Just in time for delivery, too. Let's introduce them to the others.

Leda was nearest him. He shoved her roughly toward the back of the cave. The others stumbled after her.

As they rounded a curve on the shelf of rock, Flavia gasped. The cave extended farther back, and the rocky shelf became a sandy beach leading down to the water. Huddled on the damp sand against the dripping cave wall were nearly fifty children, hands bound, dimly lit by the blue-green light reflecting off the water. Flavia scanned their faces hopefully, but Nubia was not among them.

Flavia wasn't sure whether to be disappointed or relieved.

■■■

It was two hours after noon when Lupus got back to the Villa Limona with Tigris and Scuto. His arms were aching. Tigris had revived but had been too groggy to walk. Lupus had carried him all the way.

The porter recognized him and let him in with a yawn. Lupus left the dogs in his bedroom, then went to the kitchens to get them some food and drink. Back in his room, he gave them each a marrowbone and filled their water bowls. Then he grunted, "Stay!"

Tigris had curled up on Jonathan's pillow but Scuto whined. Lupus knew he wanted to search for Flavia.

Lupus grunted "Stay!" again, and this time Scuto gave a deep sigh and lay down beside Tigris. Lupus patted his head.

Then he went to find the patron.

"Sit there on the sand," said Sorex, pushing Flavia roughly forward.

"I need to use the latrine," whimpered Pulchra. Her voice sounded tiny in the vast cavern.

"As you can probably smell," said Actius with a shrug, "everyone just goes in the sand where they're sitting."

Pulchra looked at him in horror. She opened her mouth to wail and then thought better of it. Instead she turned to Lucrio, who was obviously the leader.

"Do you know who I am?" she said.

The three men exchanged glances.

"I am Polla Pulchra!"

Lucrio, Sorex, and Actius looked at Pulchra.

They looked at each other.

Then they burst out laughing. Pulchra's hair was tangled and full of twigs. Her drab green tunic was ripped along the shoulder seam. Her face was grubby and smudged, with four red scratch marks across her left cheek and a smear of dried blood beneath her nose.

"That's a good one, darling," said Sorex in his high voice. "Shows real imagination!"

"Besides," said Lucrio, "I saw Polla Pulchra once, and you're nothing like her."

"Nonsense! I'm Pulchra and this is my slave, Leda. Tell them, Leda. Tell them who I am."

But Leda was so terrified that she couldn't even raise her eyes.

"So," said Lucrio, "she's your slave, is she? Let's just have a look and see how you've treated her."

He stepped over to Leda and tugged the back of her tunic neck. The slave girl winced.

"You freeborn types make me sick," Lucrio snarled at Pulchra. "Don't you realize slaves have feelings, too?"

"All of you, turn around!" commanded Sorex. "Come on Curly-top. You, too Knobbly-knees. Turn around."

They stared at him blankly, so he roughly turned them to face the children who sat shivering on the sand.

Flavia tried to smile bravely down at the wretched faces looking up at her. Some of the children lowered their eyes in shame, as if they knew what was coming. One boy with reddish hair stared back at her steadily and she felt he was trying to give her courage.

"Don't worry," said Actius to Leda, "you've been beaten quite enough. Stop crying. Maybe your new master will be kinder." Flavia saw Leda stumble forward onto the sand, as if she'd been pushed.

"Which one first?" came Lucrio's cultured voice from behind them. "Knobbly-knees, I think. You do the honors, Sorex. And try not to damage the merchandise."

There was an ominous pause.

Then Flavia felt a searing streak of pain across her back. And then another. And another.

They were beating her.

The Villa Limona seemed strangely empty. There were a few drowsy slaves in yellow, but all the dark-haired young men in fashionable sea green seemed to be gone. Lupus couldn't find

Felix anywhere. The atrium was silent and the double doors of the tablinum locked. The inner gardens and courtyards shimmered in the hot afternoon, and even the baths were deserted.

"The patron left an hour ago," said the porter. "Not sure where he's gone."

At last Lupus found Polla Argentaria sitting in her shaded portico, gazing out over the blue Bay of Neapolis.

"Hello, again," she smiled. "Sit beside me for a while."

Lupus shook his head vigorously and held out the tablet he'd been showing to anyone who could read:

WHERE IS FELIX? I MUST SEE HIM.

"My husband left for Rome a little while ago."

Lupus wrote with a trembling hand:

PULCRA IS IN TROUBLE! KIDNAPPERS.

"Sit beside me for a moment," smiled Polla, patting the yellow cushion. Lupus was exhausted, so he sank gratefully onto the chair. Polla would know what to do.

"I have a theory about my husband," she said, "that I've never told anyone before."

Lupus looked at her in surprise, but she put her elegant finger to her lip and smiled at him. "I believe," she said, "that my husband is part man, part god. Like Hercules."

Lupus stared at her.

"For a long time," Polla continued serenely, "I wondered which of the gods was his father. At first I thought it was Jupiter—or Mars, perhaps—but now I think it was Dionysus."

Lupus gave her a look of alarm and held up his wax tablet, pointing urgently at Pulchra's name. Couldn't Polla read?

"No, no," she touched his arm with fingers as cool and light as a butterfly. "Don't worry about Pulchra. The son of Dionysus will protect her."

Polla smiled and closed her eyes.

SCROLL XXI

Jonathan sat miserably on the damp sand, his back on fire with pain.

Flavia sat next to him, shivering and silent. Little Sorex had beaten her hard, too, though he had taken care not to break the skin.

"Don't damage the merchandise," Lucrio had growled repeatedly.

Poor Pulchra lay in the sand on Jonathan's other side. Lucrio had beaten her himself because she had shrieked with each blow and this had amused them greatly.

"We are the *pirates*, the *pirates* of Pompeii!" Sorex and Actius had sung, and with each "pirates" Lucrio had struck Pulchra's back. After a while she had fainted, so they dropped her on the sand and went off toward the stairs.

As Jonathan sat trembling with pain and fear and shame, he closed his eyes and prayed.

Almost immediately a thought came into his head. A thought as fully formed and solid as a pebble dropped into a bucket. "Make them laugh."

He thought about this for a moment. He didn't really understand what it meant but he knew it was something he could do. When he'd attended school at Ostia's synagogue he'd always been in trouble for making the others laugh.

Jonathan took a breath, struggled to his feet, and looked around.

Some of the children looked up at him, terrified of what the pirates might do if they came back and saw him standing. The others kept their eyes averted.

"Hello, everyone," he began, but his voice cracked and he had to clear his throat. "Hello! My name is Jonathan. Those men captured me, laughed at me, and beat me. And that makes me angry. But you know what makes me angriest of all?"

They were all looking at him now.

"What makes me angriest of all is that they called my friend Flavia here, well, they called her Knobbly-knees. And that makes me *really* angry!" Some of the children tittered and the red-haired boy laughed out loud.

Jonathan smiled down at Flavia. Her eyes were red rimmed and her face smeared with dust. But there was a gleam in her gray eyes and she awkwardly rose to join him. She turned and looked at them all.

"Hi!" she said, as brightly as she could. "My name's Flavia Gemina, daughter of Marcus Flavius Geminus, sea captain. Do you think I have knobbly knees?"

The red-haired boy called out, "You have beautiful knees!" More children laughed and Flavia gave him a mock bow.

"Tell me, Flavia," said Jonathan. "How many pirates does it take to light an oil lamp?"

"I don't know, Jonathan," said Flavia, playing along. "How many pirates does it take to light an oil lamp?"

"Three," said Jonathan. "One to light the wick and two to sing the pirate song!"

Several more children laughed at the audacity of this. Pulchra lifted her head from the sand and blinked groggily.

"Tell me, Jonathan. How many patrons does it take to light an oil lamp?"

"I don't know, Flavia," Jonathan looked at the children and wiggled his eyebrows up and down. "How many patrons does it take to light an oil lamp?"

"Only one, but he can't do it unless twenty clients kiss his . . ."

"Flavia!"

More laughter.

"You know, Flavia," said Jonathan. "I was in Pompeii last week and a funny thing happened to me on the way to the forum. . . ."

"Yes?" said Flavia

"It wasn't there anymore!" Everyone laughed at this dreadful joke, including Jonathan. The laughter made his back hurt less.

"Anyone here from Oplontis?" he said.

A few children nodded.

"Well, we won't hold it against you. . . ." The children were looking at him with shining eyes.

"Anyone here named Apollo?" said Jonathan.

"I am," said a boy with dark brown hair. He sat up straighter.

"I think you'd better go and sit with the kids from Oplontis," said Jonathan.

"Is there a Rufus here?" said Flavia suddenly.

"That's me," said the red-haired boy.

"Well your sister, Julia, and your grandparents miss you, Rufus, so I don't know what you're still hanging around here for."

"And Melissa . . ." said Jonathan. "Boy! Are you in a lot of trouble with your father!"

A frizzy-haired girl laughed through her tears.

"My name's Helena Cornelia!" cried another girl. "Have you seen my parents?"

"I'm Quintus Caedius Curio," called a boy.

"I'm Thamyris," said another.

Soon all the children were calling out their names, laughing and crying, asking for news of their parents, relatives, or friends.

Abruptly they all fell silent.

Jonathan and Flavia slowly turned to see Lucrio coming toward them. He held a birch switch in one hand and was tapping it against the palm of the other.

"Turn around," he said coldly. Jonathan turned and faced the children. Every eye was on him, so Jonathan smiled and winked at them.

Lucrio shoved Flavia. "You, too, Knobbly-knees," he sneered, and his jaw dropped as all the children burst out laughing.

Jonathan laughed, too. But he knew as the first blow landed on his back that he would pay for that laughter.

Lupus paced up and down the lower portico of the Villa Limona, desperately trying to think what to do next.

Felix was gone. Polla was obviously insane. The slaves were useless.

He had two choices. He could try to rescue his friends himself or he could go back to the refugee camp for help.

He glanced at the sun, already beginning its descent. He reckoned he had about four hours till sunset.

Finally he made his decision. In Jonathan's room he found an extra wax tablet and after a few minute's thought, he composed a careful message to Felix, in case he should by some miracle turn back from Rome.

Then he made certain he had a sharp knife, his sling and stones, his wax tablet, and a gourd of water.

He grunted a firm "Stay!" to the dogs and made his way to Felix's tablinum, where he slipped the wax tablet under the double doors.

Then, looking around to make sure no one was watching him, Lupus made his way through the villa and down the path to the secret cove.

SCROLL XXII

Lupus pulled the rowboat up onto the crunchy beach and sprinkled it with ashy sand to make it less noticeable. It had taken him longer than he had hoped to row from the Villa Limona to the crescent beach, but he still had a few hours before sunset.

Crouching behind the rocks, he studied the narrow strip of ashy beach and the cliffs that rose up from it. When he was sure he had not been observed, he slipped back into the water and swam a short distance out to sea.

He stopped to tread water and get his bearings. There were several grottoes along the waterline. Which one had the blue boat come from? Not the largest one. At last he struck out for the middle cave.

The water was cool and silky against his skin, and as he swam Lupus thought of his father.

He remembered the time they had sailed together to a neighboring island, how they had caught fish and grilled them right there on the beach and lay under the stars talking long into the night. And in the morning they had sailed home.

Lupus almost swallowed a mouthful of seawater. In his memory, the image of his father had been replaced by that of Felix. Gasping for breath, he clung to some rocks and took several deep breaths.

He must never forget his father's face. He must never forget his father's death. He closed his eyes and forced himself to remember. His father had been shorter than Felix, with straight black hair and green eyes.

After a while his father's image grew clear in his mind and his heartbeat slowed to normal. Lupus released the slippery rock he'd been clinging to and looked around. He was at the entrance to the grotto, and he could see it went a long way back. This must be the one.

He took several breaths and finally pushed all the air out of his lungs before filling them as full as he could.

Then he frog-kicked down and down, feeling the familiar weight of the water above him. Fine ash suspended in the water made it seem thick and green, so that for a moment he imagined he was swimming in a giant liquid emerald. He kept his mouth closed and his eyes open and saw a silver cloud of fish flicker and turn before his eyes. He looked up. Above him rays from the late afternoon sun struck the surface skin of the water like spears, and bled light into the emerald underbelly of the sea.

Lupus rejoiced in the water's beauty and swam on. Gradually the emerald water became turquoise, then sapphire, then lapis lazuli.

He knew he must surface for air. Luckily the rock above formed a kind of shelf. He found a place where the rock projected above the water and slowly surfaced. Quietly he filled his lungs with cool life-giving oxygen. Then he looked around.

High in the mountains, in one of the cliff caves overlooking the sea, Nubia sat stroking Nipur's silky fur and gazing out at the sunset. It was evening and though the stones of the cliff still glowed with heat, a cool breeze ruffled her tunic.

Beside her sat Kuanto of the Jackal Clan, whom the other slaves called Fuscus. He and Nubia had been sitting here all afternoon in the cool shade, talking about their desert homeland and learning about each other.

She had not intended to run away, even though Kuanto was handsome and Flavia had called her stupid. Not even when Pulchra beat her. But when Pulchra had snapped the lotus-wood flute across her knee, something inside Nubia had snapped with it.

She had taken Nipur and run out of the Villa Limona and made her way up to the shrine of Dionysis. Then she had followed the red cords on the branches. Even before she reached the cave, Kuanto had seen her and had run to meet her, surefooted as a mountain goat on the steep path.

The cave was wide-mouthed and bright, with a level sandy floor. A dozen other runaway slaves were there, cooking, weaving, chatting softly. They ranged in age from a newborn baby at his mother's breast to an old Greek with a bushy white beard.

One of the women slaves had smoothed ointment over the wounds on Nubia's back. Then they gave her brown bread and cheese and a cup of hot sage sweetened with fig syrup.

As she sat on a threadbare carpet at the mouth of the cave, Nubia sipped the bittersweet drink and listened to Kuanto speak of his life and his dreams.

He was older than she had first thought: almost twenty. Seven years ago, he told her, Arab slave traders had captured him and taken him to the slave markets of Alexandria. A Roman slave dealer had bought him and taken him to the great port of Puteoli, and there he had been sold again, this time to a rich man who owned many other slaves.

This man put Kuanto to work on his estate of olives and vines. For seven years Kuanto worked well and, as he gained his master's trust, he was given more and more responsibility.

Then, a week ago he had been traveling on business to Pompeii. Suddenly the earth had trembled and the mountain exploded. Immediately he made for the town gates. The city officials were telling people to stay put, but he ignored them. Borrowing a horse, he rode south as fast as he could.

After the days of darkness, Kuanto met other slaves separated from their masters or mistresses. They began to stay together, living in caves in the hills and stealing or buying food where they could

As he spoke, Nubia turned to look at the twelve slaves farther back in the cave. They seemed content, and all of them had hope in their eyes.

Kuanto told her his plan. He knew a ship's captain willing to carry them to the great city of Alexandria in Egypt.

Alexandria was a city of possibilities. One could begin a new life there. From there one could catch a ship to any land. From there one could follow the Nile back to the desert.

"Come with me," he said to Nubia in their own language. "Come back to the sea of sand and the tens of my clan. Perhaps some of your family survived or escaped."

Nubia nodded. "My brother Taharqo," she said. "He fought bravely but they chained him and after the slave traders came he went with the men and I went with the women. He may still be alive. Perhaps he escaped!"

"It is possible," said Kuanto.

Nubia frowned. "But how will you pay the ship's captain?" she asked. She knew that it cost a lot of money to hire a ship. Flavia's father had very rich patrons who paid for each voyage.

"My master entrusted me with a bag of gold. I was to purchase spices and fish sauce, but I never had a chance to spend it. That gold will pay for the voyage with plenty left over."

He gazed toward the horizon and said quietly, "Of course, if they catch me, I will be crucified. But it is a risk worth taking."

Nubia looked sideways at Kuanto. He had a fine nose and a sensitive mouth and his body was lithe and muscular.

"Look," said Kuanto, and pointed with his chin at the huge red sun just touching the horizon. He spoke softly in their native language. "To most a bloodred sun is a portent of doom. But those of us from the desert know differently."

He turned his tawny eyes upon her. "For us," he whispered, "the red sky is a sign of fair days ahead."

Before the pirates left the cave, they gave their fifty captives a drink of water. Then they bound Flavia's and Jonathan's ankles with leather thongs and poured buckets of seawater over the two of them. Flavia gasped as the cold salty water drenched her skin and tunic.

Pulchra was conscious now. Her voice rang out clearly as the three men walked away. "You'll be sorry one day."

The pirates did not even turn to look at her.

"Goodnight, children." Actius's deep voice echoed from the stairs. "Sweet dreams!"

Flavia heard their echoing footsteps grow fainter and fainter. The sun must have been setting outside, for the diffused light from the entrance was orange now. She struggled to untie the bonds on her ankles but they were too tight. Tighter than they had been a moment ago.

Flavia realized why the kidnappers had poured water on her. As the wet leather thongs around her wrists and ankles slowly dried, they tightened. In an hour or so they would begin to cut into her skin.

SCROLL XXIII

Nubia listened to the other runaway slaves tell their stories. They had all eaten from a communal pot, using the soft flat bread to scoop the stew into their mouths, and now, as the sun set, they spoke of their past.

The young mother, Sperata, was sixteen. She told how, when she was fourteen, she and her mistress had both given birth to baby girls on the same day. Although the master of the household had been father to both children, hers had been taken away and she had been forced to nurse her mistress's child. The baby she held in her arms—a boy—was her second. The volcano's eruption had prevented them from taking this one from her, too.

The Greek with the white beard was named Socrates. He spoke three languages and had taught the children of a rich senator all his life. Now that the children were grown and had left home, he had been put to work in the vineyards, doing backbreaking work under a blazing sun. He was sixty-four years old and suffered from arthritis.

Phoebus, a cleanshaven dark-haired man of about thirty, was also a well-educated Greek. He had kept his master's accounts until he had been falsely accused of stealing. His master had sold him to the manager of the Nucerian baths, where he had spent four years cleaning the latrines and scrubbing down walls. His poorly educated new master resented his knowledge and often beat him for fun.

Kuanto looked across the fire at Nubia.

"Do you have a story?" he asked in Latin.

Nubia swallowed. She had been well treated from the moment Flavia had bought her. Already she was beginning to miss her friends.

"No story," she replied after a moment. "But I have a song. A song of hope."

And because she had no flute, Nubia sang the "Song of the Traveler," the song her father had sung the night he died.

She sang of the young traveler who sets out to find happiness. He leaves his family in the Land of Gold, where the sun and the sand and the goats are golden. First he travels to the Land of Blue, where everything is water and fish and sky, and people live in boxes that float on the water. Then he travels to the Land of Red, where everything is made of brick and tile and the people do not move from place to place. He travels to the Land of White, full of snow and ice and frost, and so cold that people dress in white animal fur.

Finally he travels to the Land of Gray, a terrible land full of smoke and ashes and drifting spirits. He believes there is still another land, the best land of all, but he cannot find it. The young traveler grows thinner and thinner, grayer and grayer, but he never stops searching.

At last he finds the Land of Green, a garden full of fruit-bearing trees and shrubs and flowers and lush grass. A land of rivers and fountains and rain and life. He finds his family there, waiting for him. And so they live happily every after, laughing and feasting, telling stories and playing music.

The light in the grotto had turned from orange to a deep glowing red. The water was as purple as wine. Jonathan was leading the others in a chorus of *Volare!* And the fifty voices echoing off the walls and dome of the grotto made the jolly song sound ethereal, as if angels were singing with them.

Then a girl screamed.

A dripping figure in a sea-green tunic was rising up from the water.

"Lupus!" Jonathan and Flavia cheered at the same time.

Lupus slicked his hair back with both hands and grinned at them. He took out his sharp knife, stepped forward, and began to cut their bonds.

As Nubia finished her song, three men appeared in the mouth of the cave.

"What news?" said the first one, looking down at Kuanto. "Has the ship arrived?"

"Just there," said Kuanto. "Coming from Caprea with the evening breeze. She'll be in the cove shortly and we'll go as soon as the moon rises. But that's not for a few hours. Come! Sit! Have a cup of spiced wine and some stew. We've saved you some."

"Who is this?" said the first man, smiling down at Nubia. He had a narrow face and a jaw dark with stubble. "I've seen you before, haven't I, in the refugee camp?"

Nubia looked at him and then at the other two, a short man and a tall man.

"This is the girl who plays a flute like a bird and sings like an angel," said Kuanto. "Nubia has joined us in our flight to freedom. Nubia, meet the actors Lucrio, Sorex, and Actius. They're going to help us escape!"

By the time Lupus had cut their bonds and fifty children had rubbed life back into their wrists, the red light in the grotto had deepened to purple and then dark blue.

"The light will be gone soon," said Jonathan. "But in a few hours the moon will rise. I saw it last night when we finished dinner: a full moon."

Lupus nodded to confirm this.

"I don't even remember going back to my room," said Flavia. "But if you're right, it should give us enough light to escape and be far away from here by dawn."

"But where can we go?" said Jonathan. "We can't go back to the Villa Limona. Felix is behind all of this."

"Of course he's not!" said Pulchra angrily. They were sitting in a circle on a dry patch of sand. "Pater would never be involved in anything like this!"

Lupus flipped open his wax tablet and wrote:

FELIX ISN'T THERE. HE'S IN ROME.

"Ridiculous," said Pulchra. "Pater hasn't been to Rome in years. Who told you that?"

YOUR MOTHER

Pulchra was silent and stared at the sand. Finally she said, "Mater isn't well. She had a bad fever after Pollinilla was born. Ever since then she's been getting bad headaches. Sometimes she can't tell what's real and what isn't." After a moment Pulchra added, "That's why we moved here three years ago. Pater wanted to keep her safe. He hardly ever spends the night away."

Lupus looked up sharply. If Felix hadn't gone to Rome . . ."

"I'm sorry your mother isn't well," said Jonathan.

Pulchra looked at him. In the deep blue light it was hard for Lupus to see the exact expression on her face. "Pater thinks she's dying," she said quietly. "He's never told me, but I can tell. That's why last night was so special. You don't realize. . . . She gets so tired. . . ."

Flavia swallowed. "We're sorry," she said. Then she took a deep breath. "I'm sorry, too, Pulchra. I'm sorry I called you names and fought with you. But Nubia is more than my slave. She's my friend."

In the dark blue gloom that filled the grotto, Lupus saw Pulchra turn her head away.

"You're lucky to have such a friend," Pulchra said to Flavia.

"Lupus," said Jonathan. "I can barely see you or your wax tablet. Is there anything you want to tell us before it's completely black in here?"

Lupus bent his head over his tablet and wrote. Then he showed it to them:

LET'S GO TO VILLA LIMONA WHEN MOON IS UP

SCROLL XXIV

". . . and my name is Titus Tadienus Rufus," called a voice in the darkness. "I'm from Rome, but we were staying with my grandparents in Nuceria. My favorite color is red, my favorite food is venison, and the person I miss most is my little sister, Julia. Even though she can be as annoying as a broken sandal strap." Jonathan could hear the grin in his voice. "And this is my favorite joke: A butcher visited a farmer from Oplontis who bred four-legged chickens. 'My customers would love these,' he said to the farmer, 'but tell me, what do they taste like?' 'I don't know,' said the farmer. 'They run so fast I've never been able to catch one!'"

Laughter echoed in the pitch-black darkness of the grotto. It had been Jonathan's idea to talk to help pass the time and give the others courage.

"Thank you, Rufus," he said. "Next!"

"I think that's everybody," came Flavia's voice.

"No, there's one more person," said Pulchra's voice.

"I know," said Jonathan, "but it's too dark for us to read what Lupus writes. . . ."

"Not Lupus. Leda. My slave girl."

"Oh," said Jonathan. And then, "Um . . . sorry, Leda. It's your turn."

There was a long pause and then a small voice said, "My name is Leda. I come from Surrentum. My favorite color is blue, my favorite food is cod with lemon, and the person I miss most is Cook, because she gives me food when I'm hungry. And I don't know any jokes. . . ."

There was a hurried whisper and then Leda said: "How many gladiators does it take to light an oil lamp?"

"I don't know, Leda," said Jonathan. "How many gladiators does it take to light an oil lamp?"

"None. Gladiators aren't afraid of the dark!"

Everyone laughed and then Jonathan said, "And neither are we! Are we?"

Fifty voices shouted, "No!"

"Look! I think the moon is rising!" It was Flavia's voice.

Jonathan could just make out pale ripples undulating toward him on the black surface of the water. Gradually the ripples grew brighter and a faint milky pink light began to infuse the cave. Within minutes he could see their faces, pale globes in the darkness.

Flavia stood up, and gave her hand to Jonathan and then to Lupus.

"This is it," she said. "Let's get out of here and go to the Villa Limona! Come on everybody, follow me!"

"You really are bossy, aren't you?" said Pulchra, and smiled as Flavia whirled to face her. "Almost as bossy as I am."

"Don't be silly." Flavia lifted her chin. "I'm far bossier than you!"

Jonathan couldn't help smiling.

Because Flavia's only thought was to get the children out of the grotto and away as quickly as possible, she didn't think to check the cliff top first. She led the grateful children up the narrow steps toward the rosy light of a cherry-red moon. As she emerged from the secret entrance and stepped out onto the cliff top an arm roughly circled her shoulders and chest. She felt cold, sharp metal hard against her throat and heard Lucrio's voice snarl out to the others coming after her, "Get back down, you miserable lot, and if there aren't fifty of you waiting when I come back down, I swear I'll cut her throat. Do you hear me? I said I'll kill Knobbly-knees."

This time no one laughed.

His teeth chattering and his heart pounding, Lupus clung to a rough wet stone and bobbed in the dark water just outside the mouth of the grotto. Luckily he had been the last in line. When he had heard the man's voice at the top of the stairs, he had slipped back into the sea. He had surfaced to see a large merchant ship lying at anchor in the moonlit cove and its rowboat coming straight toward him.

The men on the rowboat hadn't seen him. Hiding behind his rock, he had watched the boat make several trips from the grotto to the ship and back. Now he saw the boat come out again. By the light of a torch held by the man at the front, he could see a dozen children, Flavia and Jonathan among them. This must be the final load.

Lupus knew the merchant ship would probably set sail with the dawn breeze. And once the ship sailed, his friends would be gone forever.

He must return to the Villa Limona quickly to get help.

As he pushed out through the skin of silver moonlight on the surface of the inky water, Lupus prayed that Pulchra was right and that her father hadn't gone to Rome. There was no one else he could turn to now. He knew Felix would do anything to help his daughter, if only he could be reached.

"Please, God," Lupus prayed. "Let him be there."

The moon was high in the sky by the time Nubia followed Kuanto and the other runaway slaves down onto the crescent beach. A fisherman and his rowboat were waiting to take them to a large merchant ship that floated close to shore.

Kuanto was the last into the rowboat. He pushed the boat into the water and jumped in, making the small boat rock. As he and the old fisherman pulled at the oars, Nubia shivered and hugged Nipur tightly. She was taking a dangerous step toward freedom. The journey might end in death or punishment.

She thought of all the things she would miss about this country call Italia. She would miss mint tea and stuffed dates and inner gardens and fountains. She would miss Scuto and Tigris. Most of all she would miss Flavia and Jonathan and Lupus. Especially Flavia, who had been so kind to her.

Nubia gazed up at the moon. It seemed to stare back at her coolly. It was smaller now and more remote, and its silvery light washed the sea and shore and ship, and made everything seem unreal.

She would miss Mordecai and Alma and Flavia's father and uncle. And beautiful Miriam. Nubia had no family to go back to. What if she and Kuanto couldn't find her clan? What if all her relatives had been captured by slave dealers?

She remembered her father, lying on the blood-soaked sand, and her mother screaming and . . . no. She refused to think about that. She had Kuanto now. He would protect her. He would protect her as her eldest brother, Taharqo, would have protected her.

They reached the ship. Its wooden side towered over them, now, rocking and creaking gently. One by one, the others went up the rope ladder. Kuanto handed Nipur up to a pair of reaching hands and went up himself, as nimbly as a monkey. Then he helped Nubia up the ladder and over the ship's rail. As he lowered her gently onto the deck Nubia turned. And stifled a gasp.

Before her stood dozens of children, bound and trembling with fear. Beside them men were binding the hands of Socrates, Phoebus, and her other new slave friends.

It was then that Nubia realized she had made a terrible mistake.

■ ■ ■

When Flavia saw the dark-skinned young man lift Nubia's puppy over the rail and put him on the deck she almost cried out. But she bit her lip and waited. Then he was helping Nubia over the rail and Flavia heard him say to the others, "Don't tie this one up. She's with me." He put his arm around Nubia's shoulder and Flavia heard him say, "You are with me, aren't you?"

Nubia nodded, her face solemn and composed. She was looking around the ship at the bound children. For a moment her eyes locked with Flavia's but then passed on, betraying no recognition.

With his arm still around Nubia, the dark-skinned young man addressed the prisoners.

"My name is Fuscus," he said. "This is Crispus, the patron's right-hand man, and his brother Lucrio from Pompeii. Those are Sorex and Actius. That's Captain Murex at the helm. We are the pirates," here he laughed, showing straight white teeth, "and you are are the booty! Behave yourselves and we'll treat you well. But I warn you. If you make the least lot of trouble we'll toss you overboard."

The Kalends of September dawned hazy and bright. The water was as smooth as milk and a gentle breeze filled the red-and-white striped sail, carrying the pirate ship sweetly toward the island of Caprea.

In the dark hold of the ship, the captive children stirred and groaned. The baby cried insistently, and Sperata tried to soothe him through her own tears.

Nubia came silently up the rough wooden stairs from the hold and stepped onto the deck, shivering a little in the cool morning air. Nipur followed, his claws tapping softly on the wooden deck.

She looked at the pirates, still asleep on their cloaks near the prow: Kuanto hidden under a blanket, Actius snoring on his back, Sorex curled up like a baby, Lucrio next to his brother, Crispus.

They had let her sleep on the couch in the cabin, but it had been one of the worst nights of her life.

How could she have been so wrong about Kuanto? Since coming to this new land her instincts had never failed her. Until now. She had been tricked by someone from her own country.

Perhaps it was because the more words her head understood, the less truth her heart saw.

"And where have you been?" The quiet voice in her ear made her jump. Kuanto was not cocooned in his blankets. He was standing behind her.

"I was looking for the latrine." She gave him her most solemn gaze.

Kuanto grinned. "It's at the very front of the ship. There's a place you can sit over the water and do your business. But if you don't want everyone watching, I suggest you find a dark corner in the hold. It stinks down there anyway."

Nubia nodded. "I did."

Kuanto showed his beautiful white teeth again. "Come, let's celebrate with some spiced wine!"

He took her hand and led her back toward the helm. Captain Murex lay asleep on a folded blanket beside the open cabin. One of his crew members held the steering paddle while another heated a pot of wine over a small brazier.

Nubia made herself smile at the sailor stirring the wine. He had a large red birthmark across one cheek.

"Here, let me," she said, taking the spoon. She stirred the wine and when she thought no one was looking, she did what she had to do. She ladled some of the dark fragrant liquid into four ceramic beakers near the pot. She handed them to Kuanto and the two crewmates and hoped they didn't notice her trembling hand.

"To freedom," she said, and pretended to sip from the fourth beaker.

"To us!" said Kuanto, and drained his cup.

"Who are you really?" Nubia asked Kuanto in their native language, refilling his cup. "Are you a slave?"

"Most of what I told you was true. I was a slave at an estate in Pausilypon. What I didn't tell you was that the estate is called Limon and it also belongs to the patron. He owns several, you know. He's as rich as Croesus." Kuanto sipped his spiced wine and stared at her.

"So you're one of Felix's slaves?"

"I'm his freedman. The patron recruited me to be one of his soldiers, so now I work for him. Crispus is his second in command. Our job was to keep law and order among his many clients. That mainly meant catching runaway slaves and returning them to their owners, usually to be crucified. But it seemed such a waste that we made a few changes. We started selling some of the slaves we caught to passing slave dealers. That way we make money, the slaves aren't executed, everybody's happy." Kuanto drained his cup. Nubia refilled it.

"The patron knew there would be plenty of runaways after the volcano. He told us to recruit a few extra boys for the cleanup operation. So we brought in the three actors. Lucrio is Crispus's brother, but until now he lived in Pompeii. The actors are from Pompeii, too. They lost everything in the eruption, and they were out of work anyway, so they were ready for a change of career."

"But they aren't just taking runaway slaves. They're taking freeborn children."

"That was Lucrio's idea. In all the confusion, who's going to know? They took the daughter of one of the patron's clients by mistake, but even that worked to his advantage. We returned her, and now the old farmer's forever in his debt. It was my idea to hold the rich ones for ransom. That's were the real money is."

"So Felix doesn't know about any of this?"

"Not a clue," said Kuanto. "He's lost touch with operations since he took up residence at that floating palace. Too busy composing poetry, if you ask me. But he built a good common structure. When Crispus says the patron has given him an order people tend not to question it."

Nubia stirred the wine thoughtfully and when little Sorex and big Actius came up, yawning and rubbing their eyes, she ladled some into beakers and handed them each a drink.

"What a nice start to the day." Sorex slurped his drink noisily. "Being served spiced wine by a dusky beauty. Lucrio! Wake up! It's time to have your morning cup and take inventory."

As Nubia served Lucrio and Crispus, Sorex and Actius led the kidnapped children and the runaway slaves up from the hold.

"Over there! Stand by the rail!" squeaked Sorex, and pushed them across the deck. Soon they stood, wrists bound, shivering against the ship's starboard rail.

Captain Murex was awake now, too. He and his crew sipped their wine and watched the show.

Crispus went to the end of the line, wine cup in one hand and a birch switch in the other.

"Name?"

"Jonathan ben Mordecai."

"Where are you from?" growled Crispus in his deep voice.

"Ostia."

"Are your parents or relatives rich enough to pay a ransom for you?"

"I think so. . . . We own a house. . . ."

"Good enough. Stand on the other side."

Jonathan stared at him blankly. Lucrio roughly shoved him across the deck to stand by the opposite rail.

"Name?" said Crispus, taking another sip of his wine.

"Flavia Gemina, daughter of Marcus Flavius Geminus, sea captain."

"Sea captain, eh? He should be able to afford your ransom if he charges as much as Captain Murex. Stand over there. . . ." He gave her a push toward Jonathan.

"Name."

"Leda."

"Where are you from?"

"She's just a slave," said Lucrio.

"Right. You stay here." He moved on to the next in line. "Name?"

"Polla Pulchra, daughter of Publius Pollius Felix, your patron."

Crispus's dark head jerked up and he peered at the grubby blood-smeared girl who stood before him. Then his long-lashed eyes opened wide in horror.

"Lucrio! You blockhead!" he bellowed. "You've kidnapped the patron's eldest daughter!"

SCROLL XXV

Nubia heard Kuanto curse under his breath.

"You idiot!" Crispus was saying to his brother. "How could you have made such a blunder?" His face was pale with fury.

"It can't be her," said Lucrio. "I've seen the patron's daughter. She's a prissy little blonde."

"And what color do you call this?" roared Crispus, holding up a lock of Pulchra's hair.

"I call it filthy," said Lucrio with a smirk.

"It *is* her!" Kuanto went over to them. "I'm sure of it!"

"Anyway, it wasn't me who took her!" said Lucrio. "It was Sorex and Actius. . . ."

"She wasn't acting like a noble-born girl," grumbled Actius.

"Don't blame us!" said Sorex, licking his small red lips. "You told us to grab as many kids as we could and we did. Those two were rolling in the dust, fighting like a pair of wildcats! How were we to know?"

"You fool!" Crispus ignored the actors and thrust his face close to Lucrio's. "Do you realize the power the patron has? Have you seen that thug Lucius Brassus? He'll crack your head like a pistachio shell!"

"So we give her back like you gave back the other one. Earn his undying gratitude."

"We can't do that," said Kuanto to Lucrio. "Pulchra's not some timid farmer's daughter. She's bound to talk. Then Felix will discover what we've been doing all these years."

"Pollux!" cursed Crispus. "He'll hunt us all down. And he'll never forgive me. He'll have that giant Lucius Brassus chop me up into tiny pieces and throw me to the fishes!"

In the silence that followed, Nubia could hear the hiss of water against the keel, the creak of the rigging, and the persistent cry of Sperata's baby.

"Shut that thing up!" Crispus screamed at Sperata. "I'm trying to think. Shut him up or I swear I'll throw him overboard."

Crispus had drawn the others aside for a conference. While they were occupied, Jonathan managed to catch Nubia's eye. He raised his eyebrows. Had she put the sleeping powder in the wine?

Nubia gave the merest nod of her head and looked away in case Kuanto noticed. Earlier that morning when she had gone down to the hold, Jonathan had told her about the powder in his neck pouch and she had taken away the twist of papyrus.

Now, standing on the gently rocking deck, Jonathan couldn't understand what had gone wrong. The pirates should be snoring like babies by now. He knew because he had helped his father administer the sleeping powder many times before.

Flavia gave him a sideways glance, raising her own eyebrows in question. Jonathan shrugged, then frowned. Something was wrong. Very wrong.

The pirates had come out of their huddle and were moving toward him.

They looked grim.

Lucrio gestured at Jonathan and Flavia. "You might as well join the others." His narrow face wore a sour expression. "Go on! Back over to the other side!"

"But aren't you going to hold us for ransom?" asked Flavia.

"Not anymore," he muttered.

135

■ ■ ■

"What's happening?" Nubia asked Kuanto, as he rejoined her. He folded his arms and scowled at Lucrio.

"It's too risky to ransom them now, even though it means losing hundreds of thousands of sestercii. We're going to have to sell the whole lot cheap to the buyer. On condition that he sells them in the farthest corner of the world, Britannia maybe." He glanced at her. "If the patron finds out what we did he would hunt us down, even in Alexandria."

"What will you do with his daughter?"

"We can't let her go," said Kuanto. "She'd lead Felix straight to us. I voted to cut her throat and throw her overboard but Crispus refuses. So she'll be sold with the rest of them."

"Where are we going now?" asked Nubia.

"To meet the buyer near the Blue Grotto in Caprea. As soon as we've collected the money we'll pay Captain Murex to take us to Alexandria. If we're lucky . . . if we're lucky . . . By the gods!" His eyes widened in horror.

"What?" asked Nubia, alarmed.

"Don't move!" he whispered. "Right beside you. . . sand cobra! The biggest one I've ever seen!"

Nubia's heart skipped a beat. Of all desert creatures, the sand cobra was the deadliest.

"Where?" Her voice caught in her throat.

"Right there!" Sweat beaded his forehead and his pointing hand was trembling. "Don't you see it? It's huge!"

Nubia followed his gaze, but all she could see was a rope coiled on the deck beside the rail.

There was a cry from the rigging. Nubia and the others looked up. One of Captain Murex's crewmen was flapping his arms. It was the one with the birthmark who'd been heating the wine.

"I can fly," he yelled.

He leapt into space and plummeted to the deck below.

At first Nubia thought the flying sailor was dead, but then she heard him groan. He tried to lift himself, then slumped back, unconscious. She noticed he wore a knife in his belt.

"What in Hades . . . ?" said Crispus, looking down at the crewman.

Suddenly Kuanto clung tightly to Crispus. "Cobras! Cobras!" He shrieked.

Crispus rubbed his long-lashed eyes, then widened them, as if he, too, saw the snakes. "Great gods!" he cried. "In the rigging! And there! And there! They're everywhere. . . ."

While they gazed up at the sail, Nubia bent and swiftly removed the knife from the unconscious sailor's belt. None of the other sailors noticed; they were also beginning to point and scream. There was a splash. One of them had jumped overboard.

Nubia edged over to Jonathan and cut the leather thongs around his wrists.

"I am thinking it was not sleeping powder you gave me to put in the wine," she whispered, as she cut Flavia's bonds.

"I must have taken father's mushroom powder by mistake," muttered Jonathan. "It makes people see things that aren't there."

Nubia cut Leda free and then moved on to Pulchra. For a brief moment the two girls gazed into each other's eyes; Pulchra looked away first. Nubia cut her bonds without a word and moved on to Rufus and the others.

Suddenly Pulchra screamed. Lucrio was running at them with a knife. "Vermin!" he yelled. "Rats and vermin!"

His knife embedded itself in the railing inches from Rufus's shoulder. The red-haired boy bent, grabbed Lucrio around the ankles, and flipped him neatly over the ship's side. A moment later they heard a resounding splash. All the children cheered.

"Good work, Rufus!" said Flavia.

"Thanks." He grinned and pulled the knife out of the railing. "I work out in the palaestra." He helped Nubia cut the others free.

Soon the children were running all over the deck, cheering and laughing and roaring at the remaining pirates and Captain Murex.

"Hey!" said Flavia. "It's just like the picture in the cup. The pirates are jumping overboard! Look Sorex! I'm a lion! I'm coming to get you!" She charged the little actor, roaring like a lion.

With a high-pitched squeal of fear Sorex leaped overboard, into the wine-dark sea.

Jonathan and Nubia joined Flavia. Their three heads peered over the rail.

"Is Sorex turning into a dolphin?" Jonathan asked.

"Doesn't look like it," said Flavia.

"Behold!" said Nubia. "He sinks like a stone!"

SCROLL XXVI

Flavia Gemina was tying Actius's hands together when she heard Jonathan call out: "Hey, Flavia! Your father's a sea captain. How do you sail one of these things?"

Jonathan was back at the helm, struggling with the steering paddle. "No idea!" she yelled back. Actius gazed up at her with fear-filled eyes. "Grr!" she growled. The big actor whimpered and pressed himself against the ship's rail.

Pulchra and Leda were binding Kuanto and Crispus back-to-back, winding the huge cobra rope around them.

"I found bread!" cried Rufus, coming up from the hold with a basket. The children yelled with delight and mobbed him. He laughed as they grabbed the flat disks and tore into them. It was ship's bread—brown and hard—but most of the children hadn't eaten in over three days.

Soon the basket was empty. "There's more down in the hold," said Rufus. "I'll bring up another basket."

"I'll help you," said Melissa, the frizzy-haired girl. Together they disappeared down the stairs.

"Help!" called Jonathan, wrestling the steering paddle. "We keep going in the same direction. We've got to turn around. Otherwise we'll crash into the island."

"I believe," said old Socrates, coming up to him, "that you need a man up in the rigging. Have any of you got experience as sailors?" he called to his fellow slaves. They all shook their heads at him.

"I'm good at climbing trees," said Flavia. "I'll go up!"

"I'll come with you," said Nubia.

Flavia and Nubia started for the mast. Then they stopped and looked at each other. They hugged.

"Nubia, I'm so sorry! I was horrible to you! Please forgive me."

Nubia nodded. "You are all I have now. Please don't be angry if I am being stupid." Her golden eyes were full of tears.

"You're not stupid," said Flavia, holding her friend at arm's length and looking earnestly into her face. "I meant the bulla was stupid because I was trying to impress that . . . that spider Felix."

"Felix is not the spider," said Nubia. "Kuanto is the spider. And the other one. The Crispus. He pretends orders come from Felix."

"Then Felix isn't behind all this?" said Flavia.

Nubia shook her head.

Flavia whooped with delight, and Nubia giggled behind her hand.

As they climbed the webbing up the mast, Nubia told Flavia what she had learned from Kuanto. How he and Crispus had been reselling slaves and kidnapping freeborn children behind Felix's back.

"We must turn ship around soon," concluded Nubia. "Because the buyer is waiting behind this island."

"Yes," agreed Flavia. "We have to get back to the Villa Limona. Oh, dear. The sail is too heavy. I don't think we can lift it. Can you pull that rope, Nubia? Nubia! What's wrong?"

There was a look of horror on Nubia's face as she stared toward the island. A ship was emerging from behind a cliff. As they watched, the ship's sail fluttered then ballooned as the wind filled it and pushed the vessel toward them. Both girls knew the sail well. It was a striped sail, yellow and black, like the coloring of a wasp. It was the sail of the slave ship, *Vespa*, and now they knew who the buyer was.

It was Venalicius the slave dealer.

"The little sail at the front," cried Jonathan. "I think you turn the boat with the sail at the front! But you have to take the big one in first, I think."

"I can't!" Flavia sobbed. "It's too heavy."

"Come down," yelled Rufus. "We'll try to turn the ship anyway, but it could be dangerous for you up there."

Hand over hand, like monkeys, Flavia and Nubia descended loose ropes attached to the ends of the yard. When they were a few feet above the deck they jumped.

"Now!" cried Jonathan.

Rufus undid a rope and pulled at it. The ship shuddered and tipped alarmingly to one side.

"Hey!" some of the children yelled as they tumbled head over heel. The brazier and drugged wine tipped and spilled out over the deck.

"The coals!" cried Jonathan. "Douse the coals or the ship will catch fire!"

The ship had righted itself with a groan but it had lost all momentum and there was no hope now of outrunning the slave ship.

"Jonathan, what is it?" said Flavia. "Are you all right?"

Jonathan had been staring into space. Now he turned to her and said slowly, "I think I've dreamed this."

"Well, now is not time for dreaming. It's time to do something."

"You're right," said Jonathan and began to undo the belt of his tunic.

"What are you doing, Jonathan?" hissed Flavia.

"It's my sling!" said Jonathan proudly. "It looks like a belt, but it's really a sling! Now what can I use as missiles? Something small but heavy . . ."

Nubia went to Kuanto and reached under the thick ropes binding him to Crispus. Shivering and babbling to themselves, they were oblivious to her. She pulled out a small leather pouch, opened it, and tipped out few heavy gold coins.

"Perfect!" cried Jonathan. "Now we need a way to catch them off guard. . . ." He scratched his curly head and looked around. His face lit up.

"Chickpeas!" he shouted.

Flavia and the others looked at him as if he were mad.

"Down in the hold!" he said. "I spent the night with my back against a sack of dried chickpeas! Listen carefully. Here's what we'll do. . . ."

The slave ship had drawn up alongside them. From high in the rigging, Nubia watched her hated enemy jump down onto the deck of the ship. Three of his henchmen were with him; the other two remained on the *Vespa*.

Nubia forced herself to look down at his face. Venalicius's blind eye was white and milky and swollen in its socket. The other eye, small and bloodshot, contained enough malevolence for both. His left ear was missing, and the wound was still red and weeping.

Venalicius held a razor-sharp dagger in one hand and swiveled his big head. Nubia prayed that Jonathan's plan would work: that he would see what he expected to see.

"What took you so long?" said old Socrates, putting on a good show of being irritable.

"Who are you?" sneered Venalicius.

"I'm Sorex. Actor and pirate. And here they are." He made a dramatic flourish with one hand toward thirty children, all standing against the opposite rail of the ship with their hands apparently bound behind their backs.

"I thought there'd be more," Venalicius grumbled. "Still, they're a fine lot." He walked along the line of miserable-looking children and Nubia saw him stop in front of Pulchra, who had volunteered to stay on deck. "High quality," said Venalicius, and fingered a strand of her hair. "This one should clean up nicely." He moved on. "Well, well, well! The sea captain's daughter. You're a long way from home, my dear."

Even from her perch high in the rigging Nubia saw Flavia shudder.

Venalicius nodded and looked around. "Where's Crispus?"

"Right here!" said the younger Greek slave, Phoebus, coming up from the hold. He was dark, like Crispus, and about the same height. "Where's our money?"

"Not so fast," said Venalicius. "Who says we're going to pay you?" He nodded at his henchmen, who grinned and pulled out their daggers.

Phoebus saw the knives come out and yelled the code word at the top of his lungs: "Chickpeas!"

"Beg pardon?" Venalicius squinted at him.

At that moment Flavia and Pulchra kicked over the sacks of chickpeas at their feet. As the tiny hard spheres rattled across the deck, all the children lifted themselves up on the rail.

"What the . . . ?" As one of Venalicius's big men took a step forward, his foot flew out in front of him and he crashed to the deck.

Jonathan appeared on the cabin roof and swung his sling. Another henchman fell unconscious. The cold coin that had struck him rolled across the deck.

"Don't move!" screamed Venalicius to his last man. "Stay still!"

Hoping the man would obey, Nubia took careful aim. From her perch high in the rigging she threw a terra-cotta wine jug.

It shattered on the man's head and he sank gently to the deck.

Venalicius looked up, and for a moment, Nubia's blood ran cold as he spotted her. "You!" he spat out. "One of the Nubias!"

The first henchman was struggling to his feet. He looked around blearily, saw Phoebus, and charged him again. Again he fell with a crash that shook the whole ship.

"Your guys aren't very bright, are they?" commented Jonathan, and he let fly with his sling.

A gold coin struck Venalicius in the center of his forehead. He staggered and then fell on his bottom.

"Oof!" he grunted. He sat looking blearily around, half stunned.

Nubia grabbed the end of a free rope and launched herself into space. She swung out and then down in a perfectly judged arc. Her feet connected with Venalicius's fat stomach and pushed him across the deck and hard up against the cabin wall.

"Burrf!" he gasped, both winded and stunned. Nubia dropped to the deck, one foot on either side of him, and sat hard on his chest. His horrible eyes were closed and a bright string of saliva emerged from the corner of his mouth.

Nubia wrenched the razor-sharp knife from his fingers and pressed it to the slave dealer's neck. If she slit his throat maybe the nightmares would end, not just for her but for others.

But she couldn't do it.

After a long moment, Nubia stood and stabbed the knife into the wall of the cabin and left it thrumming in the wood. Then she turned to find a length of rope to tie up Venalicius.

The chickpeas had mostly rolled to the port side of the ship. Phoebus and the children were tying up Venalicius's three men. And the slave ship *Vespa* was sailing away.

"Nubia! Look out!" Flavia screamed.

Nubia whirled to see Venalicius on his feet, staring at her in fury. One hand had closed on the handle of the dagger in the wall behind him. He was about to wrench it from the cabin wall.

Time seemed to move very slowly.

One motion of his arm and she was dead.

Then a figure with tangled hair head-butted Venalicius in his stomach.

He was down.

The knife was still in the cabin wall.

And now the children were swarming over him, tying his hands and legs and stomach until he was more rope than man.

Nubia turned and looked at her rescuer in amazement.

Polla Pulchra stood with her hands on her hips and her foot on the slave dealer's neck. She grinned back at Nubia. Then Pulchra's blue eyes focused on something behind Nubia and they widened in delight.

"Pater!" she squealed.

SCROLL XXVII

Lupus followed the patron over the ship's rail.

The boy had swum across the cove and reached the Villa Limona at dawn to discover Felix just emerging from his study with Lupus's wax tablet in his hand. Felix had not gone to Rome the day before, just to the refugee camp. Pulchra had been right.

The only ones to notice the swift approach of Felix's racing yacht had been Venalicius's two crewmen. The slave ship *Vespa* was now small on the horizon.

Pulchra ran squealing into her father's arms and Lupus allowed Flavia, Jonathan, and Nubia to hug him, too. Nipur scampered up from the hold and skittered across the deck, barking and licking everyone.

"Pater!" Pulchra cried. "They kidnapped us and tied us up and beat us and kept us in a grotto, but I head-butted the ugly one and I saved Nubia's life! Didn't I, Nubia?"

Nubia nodded and Lupus gave Pulchra a thumbs up.

Jonathan lifted Nipur into his arms and turned to Lupus. "Is Tigris . . . ?" Lupus gave him the thumbs up, too. And he gave Flavia the thumbs up for Scuto.

Pollius Felix looked around the ship in wonder. Behind him stood a dozen of his toughest soldiers, including the ugly giant Brassus.

"Lucius Brassus!" cried Pulchra, and threw her arms around him. "He's really just a big softie!" she grinned over her shoulder at the others.

"Well," said Felix, looking around at the happy grubby children and their bound captives. "Not much left for us to do! Shall we sail home again, Lupus, and leave them to it? Lupus?"

But Lupus did not hear him. He was standing over Venalicius, looking down at him. The slave dealer lay on the deck, trussed up like a pig for slaughter. His single malevolent eye opened wide in terror.

Before anyone could move, Lupus wrenched the dagger from the cabin wall and in one savage motion he brought it down toward the slave dealer's throat.

Flavia screamed as she saw the blood spurt from the slave dealer's head.

He had writhed away and Lupus had only succeeded in cutting off the top of his good ear. Now Venalicius screamed as he felt the searing pain.

Lupus screamed, too, as he lifted the dagger up and brought it down toward the slave dealer's heart.

"NO!" cried Felix, lunging forward and catching Lupus's wrist. He wrenched the knife from the boy's hand and hurled it into the sea. Then he pulled Lupus away and held him tightly. Lupus thrashed and kicked and cried out incoherently but Felix did not leg to. Finally Lupus's howls of rage became sobs that racked his boy.

Felix was on his knees now, his arms still around Lupus, whispering soothing words in his ear.

Flavia stared.

She had never seen Lupus cry.

She had never seen anyone cry like that.

"Get him out of sight." Felix said quietly to Brassus over Lupus's shoulder. Lucius Brassus nodded, lifted Venalicius with one massive hand, and took him down to the hold.

■■■

That afternoon, fifty-two very grubby children made use of the private baths at the Villa Limona. Afterward, they were given new yellow tunics to replace their old ones. Then they were fed: roast chicken, salad, and white rolls, with dried fig cakes for dessert.

Before the sun set, most of them were sailing back to the refugee camp on the patron's yacht. Felix had promised to deploy all his clerks and scribes and his vast network of contacts to reunite the rest of the children with their families.

As for the twelve runaway slaves, Felix had promised them their freedom as a reward for helping to save his daughter. If any of their masters still lived, he would pay to redeem them.

Flavia, Jonathan, Nubia, Lupus, Pulchra, and Leda were asleep before the first star had appeared in the sky and they slept late into the morning of the following day.

A strange soft muttering woke Nubia, and she stretched and yawned. She felt Nipur stir at the foot of her bed.

"Nubia?" came Flavia's voice from the other bed. "Are you awake?"

"Yes." The light that filled the bedroom was pearly gray, though it must be nearly midday.

"Lupus tried to kill Venalicius, didn't he?" said Flavia quietly.

"Yes," said Nubia. "He is hating him more than even me or you."

"I wonder why?"

They were quiet for a moment and Nubia heard the pattering become a soft wet drumming. The air smelled different.

"Nubia?"

"Yes?"

"What did Venalicius mean when he said you were one of the Nubias?"

"He was naming us all Nubia. All the girls he takes from my clan."

"You mean your real name isn't Nubia?"

"No."

148

Nubia heard Flavia's bed creak as she sat up. "What is it?"

"My name is Shepenwepet, daughter of Nastasen, of the Leopard Clan."

"Wepenshepet?"

"Shepenwepet."

"Oh," said Flavia. "Shall I call you that from now on?"

"No. I am used to wearing Nubia now. It is my new name for my new life."

The strange wet drumming outside their room had become a chuckling and gurgling in the gutters.

"What is that sound?" Nubia asked Flavia.

"What? Oh. Sounds like rain."

Nubia sat up in bed and looked at the gray sky between the white pillars of the colonnade. But it was not an ashy gray. It was a wet, fresh, bright gray.

"Rain," she whispered, almost to herself. Flavia, rumpled and sleepy, looked up from scratching Scuto behind the ear.

"Rain!" said Nubia. Scuto and Nipur lifted their heads to look at her, too.

She jumped up from her bed.

In the peristyles and courtyards of the Villa Limona, the slaves who had been commanded not to make the least noise heard Nubia cry, "Rain!"

She ran out into the colonnade. Flavia and the dogs followed her curiously and the boys came out of their bedroom, rubbing their eyes and yawning. Nubia stretched out her hand to feel the drops, but the colonnade was sheltered so she hurried up the stairs to the inner garden. The others followed.

"Rain," said Nubia, standing in the garden by the lemon tree and looking around her. A soft, steady downpour was washing the crusted ash from tree and shrub. On the mountain slopes the gray vineyards and olive trees were melting to green before her eyes.

The thirsty soil beneath her bare feet drank the rain with tiny squeaks of joy and exhaled a rich, dark perfume. In the trees the birds began singing. Nubia lifted her face to the heavens and let the cool rain wash over her. She stretched out her arms and twirled and laughed.

She had found her way from the Land of Gray into the Land of Green.

By dusk the fast, low-moving clouds were disappearing over the horizon to the southwest. The rain had washed the hills and scrubbed the sky, which was a vibrant magenta.

They had all gathered for dinner in Polla's yellow triclinium. A slave lit the lamps while Leda handed myrtle garlands to the diners. Her clean hair was pinned up with four new ivory hairpins and her face transformed by a smile.

Beneath the couches Scuto and the puppies were already crunching marrowbones. They had been bathed and brushed and were on their best behavior.

Felix reclined beside his wife, whose face was not as pale as usual.

"Patron," said Flavia, adjusting her garland. "My father told me that if you invite a slave to recline with you at dinner it means you are setting him free. Is that true?"

Felix nodded. "I believe it is. Technically a slave has to be over thirty before you can free him, but no one can enforce that."

Flavia raised her eyebrows at him to say: May I?

Felix closed his eyes and gave small nod.

Flavia looked around the room at old friends and new. They all looked back expectantly.

"Nubia," she said in a clear voice. "Nubia. In front of all these witnesses, I invite you to recline with me here on this couch. Will you accept?"

"No," replied Nubia softly.

Flavia twisted around on the couch. "What? You won't recline? Don't you want to be free?"

Nubia shook her head. "I don't want to leave you and Jonathan and Lupus," she whispered. "I have no family, no home, nowhere to go. . . ."

"But you won't have to leave us!" cried Flavia. "Whether you decide to be free or not, you will always be part of our family. But don't you think it's better to be free and stay by choice than to be a slave and have no choice?"

"Very well. Then I am choosing to be free and to be in your family." Nubia walked around the couch and solemnly reclined beside her former mistress.

Flavia took the garland from her head and placed it on Nubia's. Then they ate the dishes set before them and drank the drink of the god Dionysus.

"Nubia," said Pollius Felix, when the serving girls had cleared away the dessert course. "Now that you are a free girl will you consent to sit by me for a moment?"

Nubia glanced at Flavia, who smiled and nodded.

Gracefully Nubia rose and went to Felix's couch. She sat at the end.

Felix beckoned Pulchra, who came to his couch and held something out to Nubia.

"I am sorry I broke your lotus-wood flute, Nubia," said Pulchra. "Pater and I have bought you another one. Please accept it as a gift on the day of your freedom."

Nubia took the flute. It was made of a beautiful cherry-colored wood. She looked up at Pulchra with glistening eyes. Impulsively Pulchra bent and kissed her dark cheek, then whispered in Nubia's ear, "Thank you for saving me."

"Thank you for saving *me*." Nubia smiled through her tears.

Pulchra returned to her couch and Nubia looked at Felix, who was tuning his lyre.

"Thank you, Patron," she said.

He looked up at her with his dark eyes and nodded. "You have taught us quite a lot, Nubia, the ex-slave girl." As he finished tuning his third string he said casually, "Oh, Lupus, I believe you'll find a goatskin drum under your couch. Would you like to accompany us?"

Lupus brought forth a small drum. It was copper inlaid with silver, with a pumiced goatskin taut across its surface.

He looked at Felix with shining eyes and nodded.

"Tomorrow at noon," said Felix, placing the lyre against his left shoulder, "a warship arrives from Misenum. It will take you to the refugee camp to pick up Flavia's uncle and tutor, as well as Jonathan's father and sister. I will accompany you that far. Then the warship will take you on to Ostia. This is my gift to all of you, for giving me back my precious daughter and for opening my eyes."

Polla squeezed her husband's hand and he turned, surprised, to look at her. For a long moment they looked at one another with deep affection. Then Felix bowed his head. When he lifted it again Flavia saw that his eyes were wet with tears.

"That is tomorrow," he said at last. "But tonight . . . tonight we have many things to celebrate and to my mind there is only one way to express our joy. We will play music."

He looked at Nubia and smiled.

"You begin."

FINIS

ARISTO'S SCROLL

Alexandria   (al - ex - **and** - ree - ah)
> port of Egypt and one of the greatest cities of the ancient world.

amphitheater   (**am** - pee - theater)
> an oval-shaped stadium for watching gladiator shows and
> beastfights.

amphora   (am - **for** - a)
> large clay storage jar for holding wine, oil, or grain.

Ariadne   (air - ee - **add** - nee)
> Cretan princess who helped Theseu overcome the Minotaur;
> when he abandoned her on the island of Naxos, Dionysus
> comforted her.

atrium   (**eh** - tree - um)
> the reception room in larger Roman homes, often with
> skylight and rainwater pool.

brazier   (**bray** - zher)
> coal-filled metal bowl on legs used to heat a room (like an
> ancient radiator).

bulla   (**bull** - a)
> amulet of leather or metal worn by freeborn children.

Caprea   (cap - **ray** - ah)
> modern Capri, an island off the coast of Italy near Sorrento
> (also known as Capreae).

capsa   (*cap* - sa)
    cylindrical leather case, usually for medical supplies.
carruca   (ca - *ru* - ka)
    a four-wheeled traveling coach, often covered.
Castor and Pollux
    the famous twins of Greek mythology, special guardians of
    sailors and of the Geminus family.
ceramic   (sir - *am* - ik)
    clay that has been fired in a kiln, very hard and smooth.
client
    In ancient Rome a client was someone who received help
    from a more powerful patron; in return the client performed
    various services for the patron.
colonnade   (call - a - *nade*)
    a covered walkway lined with columns.
Dionysus   (die - oh - *nie* - suss)
    Greek god of vineyards and wine.
Flavia   (*flay* - vee - a)
    a name, meaning "fair-haired"; Flavius is another form of this
    name.
forum   (*for* - um)
    ancient marketplace and civic center in Roman towns.
freedman   (*freed* - man)
    a slave who has been granted freedom; his ex-master
    becomes his patron.
garland   (*gar* - land)
    a wreath of leaves entwined with flowers to be worn at
    dinner parties.
gratis   (*gra* - tiss)
    a Latin word meaning "free" or "for no cost".
Herculaneum   (herk - you - *lane* - ee - um)
    the "town of Hercules" at the foot of Vesuvius; it was buried
    by mud in the eruption of A.D. 79 but has now been partly
    uncovered as an ancient site.

Judaea   (*jew* - dee - ah)
   ancient province of the Roman Empire; modern Israel.
Juno   (*jew* - no)
   queen of the Roman gods and wife of the god Jupiter.
Kalends
   The kalends mark the first day of the month in the Roman
   calendar.
kylix   (*kie* - licks)
   elegant Greek flat-bowled drinking cup, especially for dinner
   parties.
Minerva   (m' - *nerve* - ah)
   goddess of wisdom.
Misenum   (my - *see* - num)
   ancient Rome's chief naval harbor, near the great port of
   Puteoli on the north shore of the Bay of Neapolis.
Neapolis   (nay - *ap* - o - liss)
   modern Naples, a city near Vesuvius dominating a vast bay of
   the same name.
Nuceria   (new - *care* - ee - ah)
   a small town near Vesuvius, several miles east of Pompeii.
Oplontis   (oh - *plon* - tiss)
   modern Torre Annunziata, a coastal village near Pompeii.
Ostia   (*oss* - tee - ah)
   the port of ancient Rome and hometown of Flavia Gemina.
Paestum   (*pie* - stum)
   Greek colony south of Sorrento, site of a Greek temple.
palaestra   (pal - *eye* - stra)
   the (usually open-air) exercise area of public baths.
papyrus   (pa - *pie* - rus)
   the cheapest writing material, made of Egyptian reeds.
patron
   a man who gave help, protection, and support to those less
   rich or powerful than himself; these clients performed
   services for him in return.

Pausilypon   (pow - *sill* - ip - on)
>   modern Posillipo, a coastal town near Naples across the bay
>   from Sorrento.

peristyle   (*pare* - ee - style)
>   a shady columned walkway usually around an inner garden
>   or courtyard.

Pliny   (*plin* - ee)
>   famous Roman admiral and author; died in the eruption of
>   Vesuvius.

Pompeii   (pom - *pay*)
>   famous town on the Bay of Neapolis buried by the eruption
>   of A.D. 79.

Puteoli   (poo - tee - *oh* - lee)
>   modern Pozzuoli, ancient Rome's great commercial port on
>   the Bay of Neapolis.

scroll   (skrole)
>   a papyrus or parchment "book", unrolled from side to side as
>   it was read.

sestercii   (sess - *tur* - see)
>   more than one sestercius, a silver coin.

solarium   (sole - *air* - ee - um)
>   a sunny room, usually in public baths, for resting, reading,
>   and beauty treatments.

Stabia   (sta - *bee* - ah)
>   modern Castellammare di Stabia, a town to the south of
>   Pompeii (also known as Stabiae).

stylus   (*stile* - us)
>   a metal, wood, or ivory tool for writing on wax tablets.

Surrentum   (sir - *wren* - tum)
>   modern Sorrento, a pretty harbor town south of Vesuvius.

tablinum   (tab - *lee* - num)
>   the equivalent of a study in the Roman house; traditionally
>   where a patron received early morning visits from his clients.

Titus   (*tie* - tuss)
   elder son of Vespasian, who became emperor one month
   before the eruption of Vesuvius.

toga   (*toe* - ga)
   a blanketlike formal outer garment, worn by men and boys.

triclinium   (tri - *clin* - ee - um)
   a dining room, usually with three couches on which adults
   reclined to eat.

tunic   (*tiu* - nick)
   a piece of clothing like a big T-shirt; boys and girls sometimes
   wore a long-sleeved one.

Tyrrhenian   (tur - wren - ee - un)
   the name of the sea off the west coast of Italy.

Vesuvius   (vuh - *soo* - vee - yus)
   the famous volcano near Naples, which erupted on August 24
   in A.D. 79.

Virgil   (*vur* - jill)
   a famous Latin poet who died about 60 years before this
   story takes place.

wax tablet
   a wax-covered rectangle of wood; when the wax was scraped
   away, the wood beneath showed as a mark; sometimes two
   were hinged together.

THE LAST SCROLL

Many people who visit the Bay of Naples to explore Pompeii make the town of Sorrento (ancient Surrentum) their base. The pretty harbor town is located on one of the most beautiful peninsulas in the world and amid lemon groves and vineyards. From here, the *Circumvesuviana* railway makes it easy to visit the cities of Vesuvius.

South of Sorrento Town on the Cape of Sorrento you will find an extremely well-preserved Roman road. Follow it down through ancient olive groves, and you will come to the remains of an opulent Roman villa right on the water. Many historians believe it belonged to a rich and cultured man named Pollius Felix. Their evidence is a poem written by a poet named Statius, a client of Felix. In his poem Staitus describes Felix's villa, which is very like the Roman villa on the Cape of Sorrento.

Farther up the coast—sheltered from Vesuvius by tall mountains—is a pretty spa town with Etruscan origins. Vico Equense is mostly built on the slopes but there is a small beach where you can still drink mineral water so full of iron that it turns your tongue red.

Also by Caroline Lawrence

The Roman Mysteries Book I:
The Thieves of Ostia

The Roman Mysteries Book II:
The Secrets of Vesuvius